PAUL TEMPLE
and
STEVE

Francis Durbridge

WILLIAMS & WHITING

Cover design by
Timo Schroeder

9781912582594

Williams & Whiting (Publishers)

15 Chestnut Grove, Hurstpierpoint,

West Sussex, BN6 9SS

Titles by Francis Durbridge published by Williams & Whiting

1   The Scarf – tv serial
2   Paul Temple and the Curzon Case – radio serial
3   La Boutique – radio serial
4   The Broken Horseshoe – tv serial
5   Three Plays for Radio Volume 1
6   Send for Paul Temple – radio serial
7   A Time of Day – tv serial
8   Death Comes to The Hibiscus – stage play
     The Essential Heart – radio play
     (writing as Nicholas Vane)
9   Send for Paul Temple – stage play
10 The Teckman Biography (tv serial)

Murder At The Weekend – the rediscovered newspaper serials
and short stories

Also published by Williams & Whiting:
Francis Durbridge : The Complete Guide
By Melvyn Barnes

Titles by Francis Durbridge to be published by Williams &
Whiting
A Case For Paul Temple
A Game of Murder
A Man Called Harry Brent
A Time of Day
Bat Out of Hell
Breakaway – A Family Affair
Breakaway – The Local Affair
Melissa
Murder In The Media
My Friend Charles

One Man To Another – a novel
Paul Temple and the Alex Affair
Paul Temple and the Canterbury Case (film script)
Paul Temple and the Conrad Case
Paul Temple and the Geneva Mystery
Paul Temple and the Gilbert Case
Paul Temple and the Gregory Affair
Paul Temple and the Jonathan Mystery
Paul Temple and the Lawrence Affair
Paul Temple and the Madison Mystery
Paul Temple and the Margo Mystery
Paul Temple and the Spencer Affair
Paul Temple and the Sullivan Mystery
Paul Temple and the Vandyke Affair
Paul Temple Intervenes
Portrait of Alison
Step In The Dark
The Desperate People
The Doll
The Other Man
The World of Tim Frazer
Three Plays for Radio Volume 2
Tim Frazer and the Salinger Affair
Tim Frazer and the Mellin Forrest Mystery
Twenty Minutes From Rome
Two Paul Temple Plays for Radio
Two Paul Temple Plays for Television

This book reproduces Francis Durbridge's original script together with the list of characters and actors of the BBC programme on the dates mentioned, but the eventual broadcast might have edited Durbridge's script in respect of scenes, dialogue and character names.

INTRODUCTION

Francis Durbridge (1912-98) began his career in 1933 as a writer of sketches, stories and plays for BBC radio. They were mostly light entertainments, including libretti for musical comedies, but a talent for crime fiction became evident in his radio plays *Murder in the Midlands* (1934) and *Murder in the Embassy* (1937).

He wrote plays and serials for BBC radio for many years, including the series for which he is best known. In 1938 he created the novelist/detective Paul Temple and his wife Steve, and when *Send for Paul Temple* was broadcast some 7,000 listeners bombarded the BBC with demands for more. Unsurprisingly Durbridge responded later the same year with *Paul Temple and the Front Page Men*, and from 1939 to 1968 there were another twenty-six Paul Temple radio productions, of which seven were new versions of earlier cases.

Then in 1952, while continuing to write for radio, Durbridge embarked on a brilliant sequence of BBC television serials (not featuring the Temples) that achieved huge viewing figures until 1980. And additionally, from 1971 in the UK and even earlier in Germany, he wrote stage plays that are still produced by professional and amateur companies today.

The radio serial *Paul Temple and Steve* was broadcast in eight thirty-minute episodes from 30 March to 18 May 1947. It was the eighth outing for Temple and Steve and the second appearance as Temple by Kim Peacock (1901-66), who appeared nine times in the role from *Paul Temple and the Gregory Affair* (1946) until the 1953 one-hour play *Paul Temple and Steve Again*. Peacock was then replaced, much to his disappointment, by Peter Coke (1913-2008) – the actor who became the definitive Paul Temple and made the role his own in *Paul Temple and the Gilbert Case* (1954) and every other serial until the concluding *Paul Temple and the Alex Affair* in 1968.

It would of course be criminal to forget the dulcet tones of Marjorie Westbury (1905-89), who performed on BBC radio as an actress and singer in numerous plays from the early 1930s and in *Paul Temple Intervenes* (in a small part) in 1942. She then appeared as Steve in *Send for Paul Temple Again* for the first of twenty-three occasions until the final serial *Paul Temple and the Alex Affair* (1968), partnering Barry Morse in *Send for Paul Temple Again* (1945) and Howard Marion-Crawford in *A Case for Paul Temple* (1946) followed by ten appearances with Kim Peacock and eleven with Peter Coke. Nevertheless, Paul and Steve notwithstanding, mention must also be made of Sir Graham Forbes of Scotland Yard, the role in which Lester Mudditt appeared on nineteen occasions from the original serial in 1938 until *Paul Temple and the Spencer Affair* in 1958.

The radio exploits of Paul Temple secured an impressive UK and European fanbase, and resulted in four cinema movies and numerous novels. In addition the Paul Temple brand spawned a syndicated newspaper strip from December 1950 to May 1971 and a television series from 1969 to 1971 (although the latter was not written by Durbridge). And on the Continent, Paul Temple radio serials were broadcast in translation and using their own actors from 1939 in the Netherlands, from 1949 in Germany, from 1953 in Italy and from 1954 in Denmark. The Dutch radio version of *Paul Temple and Steve* was *Paul Vlaanderen en Ina* (3 October – 21 November 1948, eight episodes), translated by J.C. van der Horst and produced by Kommer Kleijn, with Jan van Ees as Vlaanderen and Eva Janssen as Ina.

When in 1947 *Paul Temple and Steve* was first broadcast on the radio, the Temples had already become favourites in the cinema. *Send for Paul Temple* (Butchers/Nettlefold, 1946) was based on Durbridge's 1938 radio serial of the same name, with a screenplay by John Argyle and Durbridge, produced/directed by Argyle and starring Anthony Hulme and Joy Shelton. Then in 1948 an adaptation of the 1945 radio serial *Send for Paul Temple Again* was released as a cinema film by Butchers/Nettlefold under the title *Calling Paul Temple*, with a screenplay by Durbridge, A.R. Rawlinson and Kathleen Butler. The producer was Ernest G. Roy, the director was Maclean Rogers, and the stars were John Bentley and Dinah Sheridan.

The third Temple film was *Paul Temple's Triumph* (Butchers/Nettlefold, 1950), based on Durbridge's 1939 radio serial *News of Paul Temple*, with a screenplay by A.R. Rawlinson, produced by Ernest G. Roy and directed by Maclean Rogers, and again starring Bentley and Sheridan. And finally, *Paul Temple Returns* (Butchers/Nettlefold, 1952) was based on Durbridge's 1942 radio serial *Paul Temple Intervenes*, with a screenplay by Durbridge, produced by Ernest G. Roy and directed by Maclean Rogers, but this time pairing Bentley with Patricia Dainton.

Much later, from 2006 onwards, the BBC ensured that Paul Temple's name was not forgotten by using surviving radio scripts to re-create five of the original serials, all featuring Crawford Logan and Gerda Stevenson and using traditional sound effects plus the original incidental music pieces. The first of these, *Paul Temple and the Sullivan Mystery* (from 1947/48), was followed by *Paul Temple and the Madison Mystery* (from 1949), *Paul Temple and Steve* (from 1947), *A Case for Paul Temple* (from 1946) and *Paul Temple and the Gregory Affair* (from 1946) – all produced by Patrick Rayner, breathing new life into these serials for longstanding fans as well as those many listeners who would not have heard the originals. In respect of *Paul Temple and Steve*, the revival was broadcast from 11 June to 30 July 2010 in eight thirty-minute episodes and released on CDs (BBC/AudioGO, 2010), also included in the CD set *Paul Temple: The Complete Radio Collection: Paul Temple Returns 2006-2013* (BBC, 2017).

Unlike many of Durbridge's radio and television serials *Paul Temple and Steve* was never novelised, which makes it all the more satisfying to have his original script in print after seventy-five years.

Melvyn Barnes
Author of Francis Durbridge: The Complete Guide (Williams & Whiting, 2018)

This book reproduces Francis Durbridge's original script together with the list of characters and actors of the BBC programme on the dates mentioned, but the eventual broadcast might have edited Durbridge's script in respect of scenes, dialogue and character names.

PAUL TEMPLE AND STEVE

A serial in eight episodes

By FRANCIS DURBRIDGE

Broadcast on BBC Radio

30 March – 18 May 1947

CAST:

Paul Temple	Kim Peacock
Steve, his wife	Marjorie Westbury
Sir Graham Forbes	Lester Mudditt
David Nelson	Martin Lewis
Charlie	Kenneth Morgan
Philip Kaufman	Richard Williams
Ross Morgan	Alan Pearce
Henry Worth	Olaf Olsen
Mary Hamilton	Joan Clement Scott
Inspector Perry	Andrew Crawford
Billie Chandler	Vivienne Chatterton
Joseph	Alexander Sarner
Mrs Forester	Elizabeth Maude
Sergeant	Lionel Stevens
Ed Bellamy	Tommy Duggan
Waiter	Frank Atkinson
P.C. Braddock	Neville Mapp
Sergeant O'Day	Harry Hutchinson
Lord Craymore	Cyril Gardiner
Andros	Frank Atkinson
Narrator	Preston Lockwood

NEW PRODUCTION
11 June – 30 July 2010
CAST:

Paul Temple	Crawford Logan
Steve, his wife	Gerda Stevenson
Sir Graham Forbes	Gareth Thomas
David Nelson	Jimmy Chisholm
Charlie	Greg Powrie
Philip Kaufman	Nick Underwood
Mary Hamilton	Eliza Langland
Henry Worth	Greg Powrie
Ross Morgan	Nick Underwood
Railway Guard	Greg Powrie
Voice One	Greg Powrie
Voice Two	Nick Underwood
Voice Three	Gareth Thomas
Voice Four	Jimmy Chisholm
Inspector Perry	Michael Mackenzie
Joseph	Richard Greenwood
Billie Chandler	Emma Currie
Sergeant	Richard Greenwood
Mrs Forester	Candida Benson
Waiter	Richard Greenwood
Ed Bellamy	Robin Laing
Taxi Driver	Richard Greenwood
Waiter	Robin Laing
Lord Craymore	Nick Underwood
Sergeant O'Day	John Paul Hurley
PC Braddock	Robin Laing
Doorman	Nick Underwood
Telephone Girl	Lucy Paterson
Waitress	Lucy Paterson
Phone Girl	Gerda Stephenson
Cloakroom Attendant	Jimmy Chisholm

EPISODE ONE

THE NOTORIOUS
DR BELASCO

OPEN TO: The Villa-Rica Night Club

The dance orchestra is playing a gay, sophisticated waltz tune. There is a background of chatter: people dancing: people dining, etc. TEMPLE and STEVE are dancing together. It is early April, 1947.

TEMPLE: Don't you think my dancing's improved, Steve?

STEVE: (*Magnanimously*) I just don't know how you do it, darling.

TEMPLE: Now what does that mean exactly?

STEVE: Well, it could mean that this is a waltz and you've been fox-trotting for the last five minutes.

TEMPLE: A waltz!

STEVE: Yes.

TEMPLE: By Timothy, and I thought it was a one-step!

STEVE laughs. The music stops. There is applause.

STEVE: Come along, Fred Astaire – let's go back to the table.

TEMPLE: (*Laughing as they move off*) Of course, you can't expect me to compete with Charlie.

The dance orchestra starts up again.

Cross to PAUL and STEVE's table.

STEVE: What time is it?

TEMPLE: (*Looking at his watch*) It's about a quarter past eleven.

STEVE: I think perhaps we'd better be making a move, darling.

TEMPLE: Yes, all right. (*Raising his voice*) My bill, please.

STEVE: Well – have you enjoyed my birthday?

TEMPLE: Enormously! Don't keep looking at it, Steve – you'll wear it out.

STEVE: I can't help but look at it! It's the nicest ring I've ever seen. You are a darling!

3

TEMPLE: Oddly enough, I hadn't the slightest intention of buying you a diamond ring. I simply walked into the shop on the off chance …

TEMPLE stops talking: someone has arrived at the table.

NELSON: Good evening. How very nice to see you again after all this time.

DAVID NELSON is about forty-five. He has a pleasant, self-possessed manner. One feels, instinctively, that he is in complete control of the situation.

TEMPLE: Good evening.

NELSON: (*Laughing – but rather surprised*) You don't remember me, do you?

TEMPLE: I'm afraid I don't.

NELSON: It is Paul Temple?

TEMPLE: Yes.

NELSON: We met at a party, sir – Lord Cheswick's party. (*Jogging TEMPLE's memory*) Belfast … Nineteen thirty-seven?

TEMPLE: (*Politely*) Oh.

NELSON: You don't remember?

TEMPLE: I remember the party, of course, but …

NELSON: (*He isn't the least embarrassed*) This is the most embarrassing … Please, please forgive me, I …

TEMPLE: Perhaps the name might help.

NELSON: My name is Nelson, David Nelson.

TEMPLE: Oh. (*He doesn't remember, but his tone rather implies that he does*) David Nelson?

NELSON: Yes. (*A moment*) No?

TEMPLE: (*Laughing*) No, I'm afraid not. I'm most awfully sorry.

NELSON: Well, I suppose it's only to be expected. It's a long time ago. I'm sorry to have disturbed you, but … (*With a laugh*) you see, the waiter told

4

me that it was your birthday, and I came across
to present my compliments.

TEMPLE: Well, that's awfully nice of you but actually it's
my wife's birthday. I'm just – er – celebrating.

NELSON: Oh. (*Suddenly, amused*) Oh!

TEMPLE: Oh, but please. Please, do sit down.

NELSON: May I?

TEMPLE: This is my wife. Mr …

NELSON: Nelson.

TEMPLE: Mr Nelson.

STEVE: How do you do?

NELSON: I'm afraid I feel rather like a gate crasher, Mrs
Temple, but I remembered your husband the
moment I saw him.

TEMPLE: Ah, here's the waiter. What would you like to
drink, Mr Nelson?

NELSON: That's very nice of you – may I have a whisky
and soda?

TEMPLE: Certainly. Bring a whisky and soda, waiter.

NELSON: (*To STEVE*) Will you have a cigarette?

STEVE: Oh, thank you.

NELSON: Will you have one, sir?

The dance music stops. Applause.

NELSON: You remember the party?

TEMPLE: Yes, I remember the party quite well, now you
come to mention it.

NELSON: You spent most of your time on the balcony.

TEMPLE: (*Impressed*) Yes, yes, you're quite right, I did!
Who introduced us?

NELSON: An Australian called Charles Pekoe – he was
with the New York Times. A stout, rather
aggressive little man.

TEMPLE: (*Remembering*) Yes …

NELSON: You remember him?

5

TEMPLE: Yes, yes – I remember Pekoe …

NELSON: But you still don't remember me?

TEMPLE: I'm afraid not!

NELSON: I appear to have made quite an impression!

STEVE bursts out laughing. TEMPLE and DAVID NELSON start to chuckle. The dance orchestra commences to play a gay South American tango.

STEVE: Hello, what's this – a tango?

TEMPLE: Yes.

NELSON: Is this the first time you've been here, Mrs Temple?

STEVE: Yes, I think it is – isn't it, Paul?

TEMPLE: Yes.

NELSON: It's quite a joint, isn't it?

TEMPLE: Quite a joint!

STEVE: I wonder why they call it the Villa-Rica?

TEMPLE: *(A shrug: casually)* I just wouldn't know.

Complete FADE UP of the dance orchestra.

Slow FADE DOWN.

CUT TO: The Corridor outside PAUL and STEVE's Flat. *The lift arrives, the gates open, and PAUL and STEVE get out.*

STEVE: I thought that story Mr Nelson told us about the dog with the cold nose was one of the funniest stories I've heard.

They are strolling down the corridor towards their front door.

TEMPLE: Yes, he told it awfully well, too.

STEVE: I was surprised you didn't remember him, darling.

TEMPLE: Yes, I was rather surprised myself. Have you got your key?

STEVE: Yes … That's funny; there's a light on in the hall.

TEMPLE: It must be Charlie.

STEVE: But he ought to have been in bed hours ago.

The front door to the flat is thrown open.

CHARLIE: Good evening, sir! Good evening, Mrs Temple!

PAUL and STEVE enter. CHARLIE closes the door.

CHARLIE: It's all right, sir, I'll take the coat.

STEVE: Do you know what time it is, Charlie?

CHARLIE: Yes, it's about a quarter to twelve.

STEVE: Well, why aren't you in bed? I told you that we shouldn't be back until about midnight, but that there was no need for you to wait up.

CHARLIE: But Sir Graham's here, ma'am! He popped in about half-past ten.

STEVE: Sir Graham?

TEMPLE: Sir Graham Forbes?

CHARLIE: Yes, sir. He's in the lounge with another gent. They insisted on waiting, sir, so I made some coffee. Was that ok – (*He corrects himself*) – Was that all right, sir?

TEMPLE: Yes, that was all right, Charlie.

STEVE: Were you expecting Sir Graham?

TEMPLE: No, of course not, darling. (*Moving*) Come along, let's see what it's all about.

TEMPLE crosses and opens the lounge door. We hear the voices of SIR GRAHAM FORBES and PHILIP KAUFMAN. KAUFMAN is a man of about forty-five. He sounds sincere but he speaks with a foreign accent and at times his manner is distinctly vital. As the door opens KAUFMAN is saying:

KAUFMAN: …I agree that the situation is difficult, sir, but if you feel that my judgement cannot be trusted, then surely –

FORBES: (*Interrupting KAUFMAN*) My dear Kaufman, so far as this business is concerned, I trust you implicitly – you know that. But, nevertheless, I do feel that as a precautionary measure, we should –

TEMPLE: Hello, Sir Graham!

FORBES: Ah! So here you are, at last.

STEVE: How are you, Sir Graham?

FORBES: Hello, Steve – how nice to see you again! (*Suspiciously*) But, I say, what have you two been up to?

TEMPLE: Well, if you must know, we've been celebrating.

FORBES: So I gathered!

TEMPLE: It's Steve's birthday: she's forty-five.

FORBES: (*Taking TEMPLE seriously*) Forty fi –? (*Then he laughs*)

STEVE: Paul, you beast!

They all laugh.

FORBES: Oh, may I present Philip Kaufman? Mr and Mrs Temple.

STEVE: How do you do, Mr Kaufman – and for your information I am <u>not</u> forty-five.

KAUFMAN: I'm delighted to meet you, Mrs Temple – and you, too, sir.

TEMPLE: Thank you.

KAUFMAN: I've heard a great deal about you both.

TEMPLE: From Sir Graham?

KAUFMAN: But of course.

TEMPLE: Then don't believe a word of it!

KAUFMAN laughs.

STEVE: Charlie tells me that you've been here since half-past ten.

FORBES: Yes.

TEMPLE: I'm sorry we've kept you waiting.

FORBES: That's all right. It was my fault, I ought to have phoned you.

TEMPLE: Well, I daresay you could do with a drink. What would you like, Mr Kaufman?

KAUFMAN: Nothing just at the moment, Mr Temple.

TEMPLE: (*Faintly surprised*) No? Well – what about you – Sir Graham?

FORBES: No, no, I don't think I will, Temple – thanks all the same.

TEMPLE: Steve?

STEVE: Not for me, darling – but could I borrow your lighter for a moment?

TEMPLE: Yes, of course.

KAUFMAN offers STEVE his lighter.

KAUFMAN: Allow me, Mrs Temple.

STEVE: Oh, thank you.

STEVE takes the lighter, lights a cigarette.

FORBES: Temple. (*He clears his throat*) I brought Kaufman along to see you this evening because I felt that in view of what I've got to say to you, you might quite possibly –

KAUFMAN: (*Interrupting FORBES; quietly*) Don't you think it might be a good idea if we came straight to the point, Sir Graham?

STEVE: That's always a good idea, Mr Kaufman.

TEMPLE: What's on your mind, Sir Graham?

FORBES: Have you ever heard of a man called Dr Belasco?

9

TEMPLE: (*Faintly surprised and almost amused by the question*) You mean the notorious Dr Belasco?

FORBES: Yes.

TEMPLE: Of course I have. Why do you ask?

FORBES: (*Giving permission to KAUFMAN*) Kaufman …

KAUFMAN: What do you know about Dr Belasco, Mr Temple?

TEMPLE: Only what I've read in the newspapers.

KAUFMAN: The English newspapers?

TEMPLE: No, I once read an article about him in the New York Times.

KAUFMAN: And what did it say exactly?

TEMPLE: I'm afraid it was rather sensational. It described him as the evil genius behind an international organisation of black marketeers.

KAUFMAN: You consider that statement an exaggeration?

TEMPLE: Don't you?

KAUFMAN: I'm afraid not, Mr Temple.

STEVE: Why are you both so interested in Dr Belasco?

FORBES: Three months ago, Steve – on January 2nd to be precise – we received information from the Danish authorities that Dr Belasco had arrived in this country. On January the 10th a man called Bruno French died under rather mysterious circumstances: to be frank with you, he was murdered.

TEMPLE: I see.

FORBES: Bruno was one of the Soho boys. We'd had our eye on him for some time, but we'd never actually been able to pin anything on him. From the moment that Bruno was murdered, however, we knew that the information we had received from Denmark was right. We knew that Belasco was over here and that he had already started to form the nucleus of a new organisation.

TEMPLE: (*Interested*) Go on.

FORBES: That organisation is growing, Temple. It's growing so rapidly that, unless we can put our finger on the notorious Dr Belasco, there's going to be a new crime wave in this country: a crime wave quite without precedent.

KAUFMAN: That's no exaggeration, Mr Temple.

A moment.

TEMPLE: Why are you smiling, Steve?

STEVE: It's the Gregory affair all over again.

KAUFMAN: No! No, that's where you're wrong. You see, Dr Belasco doesn't create crime, Mrs Temple. He organises crime: organises the existing crime, as it were. There's a subtle difference.

FORBES: Take the protection "racket". There's nothing new about the protection "racket", it's as old as the hills.

TEMPLE: Good old Chicago!

FORBES: Exactly! But Belasco is organising it in this country: Belasco is putting the whole thing on a new, solid, business-like footing. Let me give you an example.

There's a grocer's shop in Soho – quite a flourishing little grocers. It's owned by a woman called Mrs Broadman. Mrs Broadman used to pay Bruno French seventeen shillings a week protection money. But she doesn't pay it any longer, instead she pays twenty-five shillings a week to an organisation controlled by Dr Belasco.

KAUFMAN: Talk to the authorities in Copenhagen about Dr Belasco, Mr Temple! Talk to them in Oslo! In Stockholm! In Prague! Ask to see the Belasco dossier. There are precisely two hundred and seventy-nine closely typed pages dealing with the activities of the notorious Dr Belasco.

TEMPLE: You appear to be quite an authority on the gentleman, Mr Kaufman.

FORBES: Kaufman is an authority on Belasco, Temple. Actually, that's why he's over here.

TEMPLE: You're from Paris, I take it?

KAUFMAN: No, I'm from Copenhagen. I'm attached to what is known as the Danish Central Bureau; it's the equivalent of your Special Branch.

STEVE: But you're not Danish, Mr Kaufman?

KAUFMAN: No, I'm a Frenchman, Mrs Temple. I was born in Alsace.

TEMPLE: Tell me: what exactly does he look like, this Dr Belasco?

KAUFMAN: I've never seen him, and to be truthful, I've never met anyone who has. In 1945 he was described by the Paris Soir as being "a short, clean-shaven, rather badly dressed little man." Two months later, the Stockholm Tagblatt described him as "a tall, elegant figure, sporting an imperial beard, and a disarming air of self-confidence."

TEMPLE: He works alone, I take it?

KAUFMAN: Nearly always, but there is sometimes another man with him. A sort of second lieutenant. A man by the name of Ross Morgan. Morgan's a Canadian. He's a tall, stoutish, rather well-dressed man. Have you the photograph, Sir Graham?

FORBES: Yes.

SIR GRAHAM takes a photo from his pocket and passes it over to PAUL.

TEMPLE: Thank you … Is this man Morgan over here with Belasco?

There's a slight pause.

FORBES: No, not at the moment, Temple.

TEMPLE: Not at the moment?

STEVE: Are you expecting him?

FORBES: Er – yes.

KAUFMAN: As a matter of fact, Mrs Temple, that's why we're here.

TEMPLE: What do you mean?

FORBES: Morgan arrives tomorrow afternoon. Kaufman's had secret information through from the Continent that Morgan intends to contact Belasco.

TEMPLE: Where is he landing, do you know?

FORBES: Yes. He arrives at Harwich.

TEMPLE: What are you going to do? Tail him back to town?

KAUFMAN: We mustn't go near Harwich, either of us.
              Morgan's smart. If he's got the slightest
              suspicion that he's being tailed, he'll never
              lead us to Belasco. Whoever follows
              Morgan back to town must be completely
              disarming. Morgan must never suspect
              that he's being followed.

TEMPLE: Go on.

KAUFMAN: I have suggested that you and Mrs Temple
              go down to Harwich tomorrow morning
              and wait for the boat. The moment it
              arrives, be on the look-out for Morgan.
              Watch him like an eagle watching a hawk!

TEMPLE: I see. You want us to be completely above
              suspicion. Just a nice, conventional couple
              returning from the Continent.

KAUFMAN: Exactly!

FORBES: What do you say, Temple?

TEMPLE: There's only one thing I can say, Sir
              Graham! (*A moment; lightly*) Let's all
              have a drink.

Play incidental music.

CUT TO: Harwich Railway Station

*The sounds of a crowded railway platform, with a distant
background of quayside noises.*

TEMPLE: (*Approaching*) Hello, darling.

STEVE: Have you seen him?

TEMPLE: Yes; he'll be coming through the barrier in
              a moment.

STEVE: What's he like?

TEMPLE: (*Casually*) M'm – more or less what I
              expected. Is the train late?

STEVE: No, I don't think so. Did you get any cigarettes?

TEMPLE: Yes. Have you got your lighter, Steve?

STEVE: M'm? Oh, yes, it's in my bag. (*She opens her bag*) Here you are.

TEMPLE: Thanks. (*He flicks the lighter and lights his cigarette*) When he comes on to the platform, Steve, I want you to turn your back on him just as if you hadn't the slightest – (*He stops*) – This isn't your lighter.

STEVE: Yes, it is.

TEMPLE: No, it's isn't – look.

STEVE: No. No, it isn't. That's funny, it was in my handbag.

TEMPLE: It must be Mr Kaufman's. Don't you remember, he handed it to you last night?

STEVE: Yes! I say, that's a bit rich! I must have used it and then dropped it into my bag.

In the background the train is approaching.

TEMPLE: It's got his initials on it … Oh, no it hasn't. It's some sort of engraving.

STEVE: It's an acorn.

TEMPLE: Yes.

STEVE: M'm – it's rather pretty.

TEMPLE: You'd better put it back in your handbag – (*He stops*) Here's Morgan. Now don't take any notice of him, Steve.

STEVE: (*Softly*) All right.

As the train pulls in, a guard calls down the platform.

GUARD: London Train. London Train. First class passengers in the rear coach, please …

Play incidental music.

CUT TO: A First-Class Compartment.

The train is speeding along.

MORGAN: (*Pleasantly; a Canadian accent*) I beg your pardon!

TEMPLE: Yes?

MORGAN: Do you think I might borrow your newspaper for a few moments?

TEMPLE: Why yes, certainly. (*To STEVE*) Darling, do you mind, you're sitting on the paper.

STEVE: Oh?

MORGAN: I'm sorry to disturb you.

STEVE passes over the newspaper.

STEVE: That's quite all right.

MORGAN: I don't know what you folks think, but it seems to me to be mighty cold on this side of the channel.

STEVE: My feet are frozen!

TEMPLE: I'm afraid there isn't any heat on in this compartment.

A slight pause.

MORGAN: (*With a chuckle*) Did you enjoy the crossing?

STEVE: I don't think I exactly enjoyed it!

MORGAN: I should say not! What time is this train due in, do you know?

TEMPLE: Well, if we're on time, we should be –

As TEMPLE speaks there is an ominous and terrifying screeching of brakes.

MORGAN: What is it?

STEVE: Paul!

TEMPLE: My God, the train's going to …

STEVE screams as the train crashes headlong into a local express. It is a railway accident of the first magnitude. The impact is terrific: the collapse of coaches: the smashing

16

and tearing of wood: steam escaping: people screaming for help: hysterical voices: a chaotic flood of noise and confusion. Men can be heard along the line.

PAUL is desperately trying to find STEVE in the wrecked carriage. There is falling wood and metal as he pushes through the debris.

TEMPLE: Steve? … Steve? (*He sees her*) Steve, darling!

STEVE: I'm all right – just a bit shaken.

TEMPLE: Now take it easy, take it easy … we've got to get out of here.

STEVE: The coach is over on its side! Goodness, we're – Paul, there's another train! We must have smashed into another train!

TEMPLE: Now don't panic, darling. It's all right. Give me your hand. Come on. Come on! Give me your hand! That's it.

TEMPLE pushes aside another obstruction.

TEMPLE: Now … you'll have to get through here – can you manage it? Take it gently, take it gently.

STEVE: Oh, look, Paul … there's someone underneath that –

TEMPLE: Yes, I know! I know! It's Morgan … I'll attend to him in a minute, I want to get you out of here first. Now, look, stand on my knees and … That's it! Now … get … hold of that girder … Get hold of the girder, Steve – that's – that's the idea! (*Straining*) That's it! There!

STEVE climbs out of the carriage. On a rush of ambulance bells and voices we follow her outside to:

17

CUT TO: The Trackside.

VOICE 1:   Take that stretcher down to the last coach!

VOICE 2:   Get some help up here!

VOICE 3:   Get me a rope! We've got to have a rope!

VOICE 4:   Stand clear! Stand clear!

Mix to where STEVE is trying to regain her breath.
TEMPLE arrives.

TEMPLE: Are you all right now, Steve?

STEVE: Yes … What about Morgan?

A moment.

TEMPLE: He's dead.

STEVE: Oh, poor man.

TEMPLE: There was nothing I could do. He was
              trapped. I tried to get him out, but it was
              no use, darling.

STEVE: Did you speak to him?

TEMPLE: Yes … Yes, I told him who I was … I felt
              I had to. He said he had an appointment
              with a man in Soho who runs a café. A
              man called Henry Worth.

STEVE: Is Henry Worth Dr Belasco?

TEMPLE: I don't know … I don't know, Steve.

STEVE: Paul, what is it? You're worried about
              something … What is it, darling?

TEMPLE: I searched his pockets. I found this
              cigarette lighter on him.

STEVE: Well?

TEMPLE: It's exactly the same as the one you found
              in your handbag.

Play incidental music.

CUT TO: Worth's Café in Shop.

There are not too many people in the café. We can hear a
distant piano.

TEMPLE: Let's sit down, Steve – there's a table over here.

STEVE: (*Quietly*) Are you sure this is the right place?

TEMPLE: Yes, I think so.

STEVE: I'm not very impressed, darling.

TEMPLE: Neither am I; but I bet a fiver our friend Mr Worth has a pretty good business.

They reach the table.

STEVE: Did you tell Sir Graham that we were coming here?

TEMPLE: As a matter of fact, it was his idea.

STEVE: Oh, I see.

A moment. The piano stops playing. There is scattered applause.

TEMPLE: (*Brightly*) What would you like? A cup of tea – a sandwich – or something?

STEVE: (*After a moment's hesitation*) Paul …

TEMPLE: Yes?

STEVE: Are we going to get mixed up in this Belasco affair?

TEMPLE: Are we?

STEVE: What do you mean?

TEMPLE: It's up to you.

STEVE: I don't want to. I don't want any part of it, darling – (*She stops*) – Paul …

TEMPLE: Well?

A slight pause.

STEVE: That girl over there – the waitress – the one serving coffee. Haven't I seen her before somewhere?

TEMPLE: Yes … Yes, by Timothy, you have! (*Surprised*) That's Mary Hamilton.

STEVE: Mary Hamilton?

TEMPLE: You remember Mary Hamilton! The enquiry agent: specialises in divorce cases.

STEVE: Yes. Yes, of course. But what's she doing here? What's she doing here working as … as a waitress.

TEMPLE: Look out. Here she is …

MARY HAMILTON approaches. She has a faintly unpleasant manner with a slightly cockney accent.

MARY: What can I get you?

MARY removes cups and saucers from the table.

TEMPLE: Can we have any sandwiches?

MARY: Yes, but they'll have to be cheese. The pressed-beef is off.

TEMPLE: All right: some sandwiches and some coffee.

MARY: O.K.

TEMPLE: (*Apparently an afterthought*) Oh, and is Mr Worth about?

MARY: I expect so. He usually is.

TEMPLE: Well, I'd like a word with him.

A tiny pause.

MARY: All right. What name shall I say?

TEMPLE: Just say … I'd like a word with him.

MARY: He's a bit fussy, you know, Mr Worth. He doesn't talk to every Tom, Dick and Harry.

TEMPLE: I'm a bit particular myself.

A moment.

MARY: All right – I'll tell him.

TEMPLE: (*Quietly*) Thank you, Mary.

MARY: If you feel you must be familiar the name is Ivy. Ivy Brown.

TEMPLE: Not one of the Berkshire Browns?

MARY: (*After a pause: not amused*) I'll tell Mr Worth.

As Mary leaves, the piano starts to play again.

STEVE: Did she recognise you?

TEMPLE: What do you think?

STEVE: I think she did.

TEMPLE: She recognised me all right.

STEVE: I wonder what she's doing here?

TEMPLE: Well, she's obviously not here for the good of her health. I know Mary Hamilton – she's a smart girl.

STEVE: Who's this? Is it Worth?

TEMPLE: (*Softly*) Yes, I should imagine it is. I saw her speak to him.

STEVE: He's much younger than I expected.

TEMPLE: Yes ...

A moment.

HENRY WORTH arrives at the table. He is an Austrian: a man of about thirty-two or three. His manner is cold and impersonal.

WORTH: You wanted to see me?

TEMPLE: (*With the faintest suggestion of a Canadian accent*) Mr Worth?

WORTH: Yes?

TEMPLE: My name is Morgan – Ross Morgan.

Pause.

WORTH: Well?

TEMPLE: Doesn't that name convey anything to you?

WORTH: No. Is there any particular reason why it should?

TEMPLE: (*Watching WORTH*) I was told to get in touch with you by Dr Belasco.

WORTH: Dr ... Belasco?

TEMPLE: Yes.

WORTH: (*With a little laugh*) I think there must be some mistake. I've never heard of your friend ... Dr Belasco.

TEMPLE: Isn't that rather strange?

21

WORTH: What do you mean?

TEMPLE: My instructions were to contact you immediately on arrival. I was told that you would take me direct to Dr Belasco!

WORTH: I find that interesting. Perhaps, however, you would be so kind as to explain something to me? (*Suddenly annoyed*) How can I take you direct to someone I've not even heard of? Incidentally, your name is not Ross Morgan. It's Paul Temple: I recognised you the moment you came into the café.

TEMPLE: (*Brightly*) Did you? Did you, by Jove!

WORTH: You see, I have a remarkably good memory for faces, Mr Temple. Goodnight.

TEMPLE: (*Faintly taken aback*) Goodnight.

WORTH leaves. A moment.

STEVE: That, I believe, is what is technically known as 'getting the bird'.

TEMPLE: The bird! I've got a shrewd suspicion he handed me the flock.

STEVE laughs.

FADE Up of café noises and the piano from the background.

FADE SCENE.

CUT TO: The TEMPLES' Car.

TEMPLE and STEVE are on their way back to the flat. TEMPLE is driving.

STEVE: Do you think he was telling the truth, Paul?

TEMPLE: Who? Worth?

STEVE: Yes. I've been thinking about that girl – Mary Hamilton. We mustn't jump to conclusions, darling. We mustn't think that just because she's working at the café, she's necessarily mixed up in the Belasco affair.

TEMPLE: Well, if she's not, what's she doing there?

STEVE: It is possible I suppose that she might be investigating a perfectly ordinary, routine divorce case.

TEMPLE: Yes, she might be; on the other hand, she might not.

Pause.

STEVE: It's the cigarette lighters that puzzle me. The one you showed me – the one you found on Ross Morgan – it's identically the same as the one in my handbag.

TEMPLE: Yes.

STEVE: Do you think that the engraving – the acorn, I mean – do you think it's a sort of – well – symbol?

TEMPLE: I suppose it must be, but if it's a symbol, then what exactly is it a symbol of?

STEVE: I don't know …

The car continues.

TEMPLE: It's cold tonight.

STEVE: Yes, I'm frozen.

TEMPLE: There's a rug on the back seat, Steve.

STEVE: Right.

TEMPLE: Of course, you know, it's my opinion that if this so-called Dr Belasco is really – (*He stops*) Steve, what is it?

STEVE: Darling, pull up! Pull up! There's someone on the floor … at the back of the car.

TEMPLE: On the floor?

STEVE: Yes … Yes … I … I felt them with my hand when I … I … Paul, stop the car. Stop the car, darling!

The car draws quickly to a standstill.

TEMPLE: Switch the light on … (*STEVE does so*)
That's it …

STEVE gives a quick, frightened gasp.

TEMPLE: Good Lord.

STEVE: It's … Mary Hamilton!

TEMPLE: Yes … and she's dead.

Play incidental music.

CUT TO: The TEMPLES' Hallway.

The front door buzzer sounds. CHARLIE approaches and opens the door.

CHARLIE:Good evening, sir. Good evening, Mrs T.

PAUL and STEVE enter.

TEMPLE: Any messages, Charlie?

CHARLIE:No, sir. But there's a gentleman here, sir. He called about five minutes ago. A Mr Nelson.

STEVE: Mr Nelson?

CHARLIE:Yes, Ma'am.

STEVE: (*To TEMPLE, quietly*) What on earth does <u>he</u> want, I wonder?

TEMPLE: Where is he, Charlie?

CHARLIE:In the lounge, sir.

TEMPLE: (*Moving off*) Right …

Cross to the lounge. The door opens and PAUL enters.

NELSON: (*Pleasantly*) Ah! So here you are!

TEMPLE: Hello, Mr Nelson! What can I do for you?

NELSON: Well, I'm sorry to trouble you, Mr Temple, especially at this time of night, but – well – (*With a disarming little laugh*) – I think your wife has … got my cigarette lighter.

TEMPLE: (*Politely*) Your cigarette lighter?

NELSON: Yes. I offered Mrs Temple a cigarette last night at the Villa-Rica and I believe I put my lighter down on the table. One of the waiters said that he thought he saw Mrs Temple put it into her handbag.

TEMPLE: (*With a little laugh*) Well, yes, as a matter of fact, I believe she did. My wife's terribly absent-minded these days, I'm afraid. If you'll just wait – (*The door opens*) Oh, here you are, Steve.

STEVE: Hello, Mr Nelson!

NELSON: Good evening, Mrs Temple!

TEMPLE: Darling, have you got that cigarette lighter? (*Significantly*) The one we thought belonged to Mr Kaufman?

STEVE: Why, yes. (*She opens her handbag*) Here it is.

TEMPLE: Is this your lighter, Mr Nelson?

NELSON: Yes, that's the one all right. (*Amused*) You must have picked it up off the table, Mrs Temple, without thinking.

STEVE: Yes, of course! Of course, I did! I remember now. How stupid of me … Then it's your lighter, Mr Nelson?

NELSON: Yes, I'm rather afraid it is.

TEMPLE: It's got rather a curious design on it. We found it rather intriguing.

NELSON: You mean the acorn? (*Examining the lighter*) Yes – yes, I've often wondered if it had any particular significance.

TEMPLE: Where did you buy the lighter, Mr Nelson?

NELSON: As it happens, I didn't buy it. It belonged to my wife. But why are you so curious about the lighter? I know it's a rather unusual one, but surely …

TEMPLE: It's not quite so unusual as you'd imagine.

NELSON: No?

TEMPLE: No. Take a look at this.

TEMPLE takes MORGAN's lighter from his pocket.

A moment.

NELSON: Why – it's – just the same! It's got the same design on it, exactly.

TEMPLE: Yes … exactly.

Closing music.

END OF EPISODE ONE

EPISODE TWO

27A BERKELEY HOUSE PLACE

OPEN TO:

ANNOUNCER: Paul Temple, the celebrated novelist and private detective, is visited by an old friend of his, Sir Graham Forbes of Scotland Yard, and by a Mr Philip Kaufman, who is temporarily attached to the Special Branch. Kaufman tells Paul Temple about a notorious criminal known as Dr Belasco.

FLASHBACK TO: The TEMPLES' Lounge.

KAUFMAN: You see, Dr Belasco doesn't create crime, Mrs Temple. He organises crime: organises the existing crime, as it were. There's a subtle difference.

FORBES: Take the protection "racket". There's nothing new about the protection "racket", it's as old as the hills.

TEMPLE: Good old Chicago!

FORBES: Exactly! But Belasco is organising it in this country: Belasco is putting the whole thing on a new, solid, business-like footing. Let me give you an example. There's a grocer's shop in Soho – quite a flourishing little grocers. It's owned by a woman called Mrs Broadman. Mrs Broadman used to pay Bruno French seventeen shillings a week protection money. But she doesn't pay it any longer, instead she pays twenty-five shillings a week to an organisation controlled by Dr Belasco.

KAUFMAN: Talk to the authorities in Copenhagen about Dr Belasco, Mr Temple! Talk to

29

them in Oslo! In Stockholm! In Prague! Ask to see the Belasco dossier. There are precisely two hundred and seventy-nine closely typed pages dealing with the activities of the notorious Dr Belasco.

TEMPLE: (*Thoughtfully*) Belasco works alone, I take it?

KAUFMAN: Nearly always, but there is sometimes another man with him. A man by the name of Ross Morgan.

STEVE: Is Morgan over here?

KAUFMAN: Morgan arrives tomorrow afternoon, Mrs Temple – and I have suggested to Sir Graham that you and your husband go down to Harwich tomorrow morning and wait for the boat. The moment it docks, be on the look-out for Morgan. Watch him like an eagle watching a hawk!

Play Incidental Music.
FADE SCENE.

ANNOUNCER: The following afternoon, however, there is a railway accident and Ross Morgan is killed. Temple searches the body and discovers a cigarette lighter: the lighter appears to be identically the same as one which Steve possesses, but which they have reason to believe belongs to Philip Kaufman. Later the same night, when Temple and Steve return to their flat, they discover that a casual acquaintance of theirs, a man by the name of David Nelson has called.

CUT TO: The TEMPLES' Hallway.

CHARLIE: Good evening, sir. Good evening, Mrs T.

PAUL and STEVE enter.

TEMPLE: Any messages, Charlie?

CHARLIE: No, sir. But there's a gentleman here, sir. He called about five minutes ago. A Mr Nelson.

STEVE: Mr Nelson?

CHARLIE: Yes, Ma'am.

STEVE: (*To TEMPLE, quietly*) What on earth does he want, I wonder?

TEMPLE: Where is he, Charlie?

CHARLIE: In the lounge, sir.

TEMPLE: (*Moving off*) Right …

Cross to the lounge. The door opens and PAUL enters.

NELSON: (*Pleasantly*) Ah! So here you are!

TEMPLE: Hello, Mr Nelson! What can I do for you?

NELSON: Well, I'm sorry to trouble you, Mr Temple, especially at this time of night, but – well – (*With a disarming little laugh*) – I think your wife has … got my cigarette lighter.

TEMPLE: (*Politely*) Your cigarette lighter?

NELSON: Yes. I offered Mrs Temple a cigarette last night at the Villa-Rica and I believe I put my lighter down on the table. One of the waiters said that he thought he saw Mrs Temple put it into her handbag.

TEMPLE: (*With a little laugh*) Well, yes, as a matter of fact, I believe she did. My wife's terribly absent-minded these days, I'm afraid. If you'll just wait – (*The door opens*) Oh, here you are, Steve.

STEVE: Hello, Mr Nelson!

NELSON: Good evening, Mrs Temple!

TEMPLE: Darling, have you got that cigarette lighter? (*Significantly*) The one we thought belonged to Mr Kaufman?

STEVE: Why, yes. (*She opens her handbag*) Here it is.

TEMPLE: Is this your lighter, Mr Nelson?

NELSON: Yes, that's the one all right. (*Amused*) You must have picked it up off the table, Mrs Temple, without thinking.

STEVE: Yes, of course! Of course, I did! I remember now. How stupid of me … Then it's your lighter, Mr Nelson?

NELSON: Yes, I'm rather afraid it is.

TEMPLE: It's got rather a curious design on it. We found it rather intriguing.

NELSON: You mean the acorn? (*Examining the lighter*) Yes – yes, I've often wondered if it had any particular significance?

TEMPLE: Where did you buy the lighter, Mr Nelson?

NELSON: As it happens, I didn't buy it. It belonged to my wife.

TEMPLE: Have you any idea where she got it from?

NELSON: No, I'm afraid I haven't.

TEMPLE: Could you find out?

NELSON: I doubt it very much. You see … my wife committed suicide just over two months ago.

TEMPLE: Oh, I'm sorry.

NELSON: But why are you so curious about the lighter? I know it's a rather unusual one, but surely …

TEMPLE: It's not quite so unusual as you'd imagine.

NELSON: No?

TEMPLE: No. Take a look at this.

TEMPLE takes MORGAN's lighter from his pocket.
A moment.

NELSON: Why – it's – just the same! It's got the same design on it, exactly.

TEMPLE: Yes … exactly.

NELSON: Where did you get that lighter?

TEMPLE: I got it from a man called Ross Morgan.

NELSON: Ross Morgan?

TEMPLE: Yes. (*Watching NELSON*) Does the name convey anything to you, Mr Nelson?

NELSON: No, no, I'm afraid it doesn't.

TEMPLE: Morgan was a Canadian. We travelled down to town together this afternoon from Harwich. But there was a railway accident and Morgan was killed. I searched the body and discovered this cigarette lighter. Ross Morgan was a friend – one might almost say an associate – of a certain Dr Belasco.

NELSON: (*Softly: obviously surprised*) Dr Belasco!

TEMPLE: You've heard of Dr Belasco, I take it?

NELSON: Yes, I've heard of Dr Belasco – (*He stops, thoughtfully*) That's odd! I've only heard that name mentioned once before in my life but I've – never forgotten it. I heard it one evening, just after dinner, about three months ago. I was going upstairs to my bedroom when I heard my wife on the telephone. She was in the library. She sounded worried and terribly unhappy. I don't know who she was talking to, but as I passed the library door, I distinctly heard the name Belasco – Dr Belasco. When I saw her at breakfast the next morning, I asked her about it, and she said that I must have been mistaken and that she knew of no one called Dr Belasco.

STEVE: Mr Nelson?

NELSON: Yes, Mrs Temple?

STEVE: I wonder if you'll forgive me if I ask a … a rather personal question? Why did you wife commit suicide?

NELSON: I don't know why she committed suicide, Mrs Temple. I've tried to find out; I've done my damnedest to find out; I've even employed a private investigator, but it was no use. Rene … my wife was always a temperamental, moody sort of a person, but somehow – I think she must have had – a very sound reason for doing what she did.

TEMPLE: Do you think she was being blackmailed?

NELSON: I don't know. I suggested that possibility to Mary Hamilton but she –

STEVE: To Mary Hamilton!

NELSON: (*Taken aback*) Yes.

TEMPLE: Was Mary Hamilton the private detective you mentioned? The person you engaged to find out why your wife committed suicide?

NELSON: (*Puzzled by TEMPLE's tone*) Yes.

TEMPLE: What did she find out exactly?

NELSON: Look here, do you know Mary Hamilton?

TEMPLE: What did she find out, Mr Nelson?

A slight pause.

NELSON: She found out what I already knew, or at any rate, suspected.

TEMPLE: What was that?

NELSON: … She found out that Rene had been mixing with – well – rather a peculiar crowd of people.

TEMPLE: What sort of people?

NELSON: Oh … Well, there was a woman called Mrs Forester. A widow.

STEVE: Mrs Guy Forester?

NELSON: Yes.

TEMPLE: Go on, Nelson.

NELSON: She used to give a lot of parties – I suppose she still does for that matter. Rene was quite a friend of Mrs Forester's. She frequently used to go and stay with her for weekends.

TEMPLE: Was Mary Hamilton under the impression that Mrs Forester had had something to do with your wife's suicide?

NELSON: Yes, I suppose she must have been. She certainly asked me quite a lot of questions about Mrs Forester, the last time we met.

TEMPLE: What sort of questions?

NELSON: She wanted to know whether I was a friend of hers.

TEMPLE: Are you?

NELSON: Good Lord, no!

STEVE: Do you think it's possible that Mrs Forester gave your wife the cigarette lighter?

NELSON: (*Rather impressed*) Yes – yes, quite possible. I know she very often did give Rene presents. I hadn't thought of that.

TEMPLE: When did you last see Mary Hamilton?

NELSON: Just over a week ago.

TEMPLE: Did she tell you whether she was making any progress or not?

NELSON: No. Beyond asking the questions about Mrs Forester she was rather non-committal. As a matter of fact, I've got an appointment to see her tomorrow afternoon.

TEMPLE: I shall be surprised if she keeps it, Mr Nelson.

NELSON: What do you mean?

TEMPLE: She's dead.

NELSON: Dead! What do you mean – dead?

TEMPLE: She was murdered.

NELSON: Murdered? I don't believe it! I just don't believe it! You're joking! You're just trying to … (*Alarmed now*) What happened?

TEMPLE: Early this evening my wife and I went to a café in Soho. We had reason to believe that the proprietor of the café, a man called Henry Worth, had information concerning a certain person that we were … particularly interested in. Rather to our surprise, we discovered that a private enquiry agent – Mary Hamilton, in fact – was working at the café as a waitress.

NELSON: As a waitress?

TEMPLE: Yes.

NELSON: But why on earth should she be doing that? … Mr Temple, who was that certain person that you were particularly interested in – Dr Belasco?

TEMPLE: (*Watching NELSON*) Yes …

NELSON: That's what I thought. Look here! Don't you think it's possible that Mary Hamilton discovered that the mysterious Dr Belasco was responsible for my wife's death, and she was trying to find out – probably from Henry Worth himself – the real identity of Belasco?

TEMPLE: Yes, it's possible.

NELSON: And supposing …

TEMPLE: Yes? Supposing what?

NELSON: Supposing Mary Hamilton discovered that Dr Belasco was a woman – supposing, in fact, she discovered that Dr Belasco was none other than Mrs Forester!

TEMPLE: Well?

NELSON: Well – wouldn't that explain why she was murdered?

TEMPLE:	Well, you can say the same thing about Henry Worth.
STEVE:	(*With a little laugh*) Or yourself for that matter, Mr Nelson.
NELSON:	… Yes. Yes, I suppose you could. Mr Temple?
TEMPLE:	Yes?
NELSON:	Who is Dr Belasco?
TEMPLE:	I don't know – yet.
NELSON:	What does that mean?
STEVE:	It means we're going to find out, Mr Nelson.

Play Incidental Music.

CUT TO: A Conference Room at Scotland Yard.

The voices of SIR GRAHAM FORBES, PHILIP KAUFMAN, PAUL TEMPLE and INSPECTOR PERRY. The voices are friendly, but there is a faint suggestion of irritation.

FORBES:	(*Raising his voice: with authority*) But it's no good arguing the point, Kaufman. You've seen the doctor's report, you've seen the report from Professor Harvingdale, and you've heard what Mr Temple has had to say about it. The position, therefore, to my way of thinking, is really this –
KAUFMAN:	(*Interrupting FORBES*) But, Sir Graham, if the girl was murdered in the café, and then deliberately taken –
FORBES:	What do you mean 'if'? Of course, she was murdered in the café!
KAUFMAN:	(*Calmly*) I disagree.
FORBES:	What do you mean?

TEMPLE:	Mr Kaufman means that it's quite possible that Mary Hamilton was murdered after she left the café. In which case my car was probably the most convenient place to dump the body.
FORBES:	But what about the medical report?
KAUFMAN:	The medical report states that the girl had been dead the best part of forty minutes! I know! Therefore, if you attach supreme importance to the medical report, quite obviously you are right, Sir Graham, and the girl was murdered in the café. Personally, however, I don't think so.
TEMPLE:	You don't?
KAUFMAN:	No.
FORBES:	M'm.
TEMPLE:	Well, I suppose strictly speaking this is your pigeon, Inspector Perry. Have you seen Mr Worth?
PERRY:	Yes, I saw him this morning.
TEMPLE:	What did he say?
PERRY:	Precisely what you'd expect him to say. That the girl left the café shortly after she served you. Apparently, the staff take it in turns to take an early evening off.
TEMPLE:	Did he know that her name was Mary Hamilton and that she was a private enquiry agent?
PERRY:	He says not.
TEMPLE:	How long had she been working there?
PERRY:	Just over a week.
TEMPLE:	M'm.
KAUFMAN:	What's your opinion of Mr Worth, Inspector?

PERRY:	My personal opinion?
KAUFMAN:	Yes.
PERRY:	(*Bluntly*) I like him.
KAUFMAN:	(*Rather surprised*) So … You like him?
PERRY:	Yes, and shall I tell you why I like him, Mr Kaufman? Because he's got guts. He came to this country just over twelve months ago. He hadn't a bean to his name, and he hadn't a friend in the world. Within ten weeks he'd ploughed his way through a mass of red tape, bought a business, and was doing very nicely for himself.
KAUFMAN:	Is he straight?
PERRY:	Well, that's rather a leading question. He sails pretty near to the wind but then, if it comes to that, quite a lot of people do. Especially in Soho. (*A moment*) Yes, he's straight, Mr Kaufman.
FORBES:	I suppose you know that Ross Morgan, the Canadian, had instructions to contact Worth the moment he arrived?
PERRY:	Yes, I heard Mr Temple say so.
FORBES:	He told Temple that he'd never heard of Ross Morgan – or Dr Belasco.
KAUFMAN:	(*Faint note of sarcasm*) How do you account for that, Inspector?
PERRY:	I don't account for it. You asked me my personal opinion of Mr Worth and I gave it to you. I think he's straight.
FORBES:	M'm.

There is a knock on the door, and the door opens.

PERRY:	Yes, Sergeant?

SERGEANT: I beg your pardon, sir, but this letter's just arrived. It's marked urgent and strictly confidential.

PERRY: For me, Sergeant?

SERGEANT: No, sir, it's for Sir Graham.

FORBES: (*Taking the letter*) Thank you.

SERGEANT: Thank you, sir.

The SERGEANT leaves, closing the door.

FORBES: Excuse me a moment.

FORBES tears open the envelope and reads the letter. A moment.

TEMPLE: Anything wrong, Sir Graham?

FORBES: (*His thoughts elsewhere*) M'm? (*Suddenly*) Er – no … Inspector, tell me: do you know a man called Marx?

PERRY: Marx? (*Surprised*) Harry Marx, sir?

FORBES: Yes. Well, at least he signs himself H. Marx. It'll be the same man, I expect.

PERRY: Oh, I know Harry Marx all right. (*A little laugh*) I expect you do too, Mr Temple?

TEMPLE: (*Quietly*) Yes, I know Harry Marx.

FORBES: What do you know about him?

TEMPLE: Before the war, he ran a small antique shop on the Edgware Road. The shop was a blind: he was really a 'fence'. When the war started, I lost track of him. I believe he went out to South Africa or somewhere.

PERRY: Aye. Yes, well he's not in South Africa at the moment, Mr Temple. He's back over here. He's been over here for some little time.

FORBES: What's he doing?

40

PERRY:	He's running a protection racket. According to all accounts he's got quite a nice little clique around him.
FORBES:	M'm. (*Suddenly*) Well – I'll read you the letter. "Dear Sir, I learn from a reliable source that Scotland Yard are interested in the identity of a certain Dr Belasco. If you will meet me this evening at Worth's café in Soho, I shall be pleased to place certain information concerning this gentleman at your disposal. Be at the café shortly after ten."
KAUFMAN:	(*Quickly, seriously*) You say this man Marx runs a protection racket?
PERRY:	Yes.
KAUFMAN:	Then it's perfectly obvious what has happened! Belasco intends to take him over! Marx has got wind of this and is obviously out to double-cross him.
FORBES:	Yes.
PERRY:	This might be our chance, Sir Graham, so far as Belasco is concerned.
KAUFMAN:	(*Faintly cynical*) You will no doubt observe, Inspector, that our friend Mr Worth once again comes into the picture.
TEMPLE:	In rather an interesting manner, Mr Kaufman, don't you think?
KAUFMAN:	What do you mean?
TEMPLE:	Well, if Harry Marx thought that Mr Worth was Dr Belasco, he would hardly suggest his café as a suitable place for a rendezvous with Sir Graham.

KAUFMAN: Yes. Yes, that's true. That's quite a point, in fact. (*A moment, impressed*) Quite a point.

Play Incidental Music.

CUT TO: Worth's Café in Soho.

The café is busy. The pianist is playing the same number as was heard in episode one.

FORBES: Our friend Mr Worth seems to have quite a flourishing little business.

TEMPLE: Yes, I think he does quite nicely.

FORBES: The place is certainly crowded tonight.

TEMPLE: There's a table over there, Sir Graham. In the corner.

FORBES: Oh yes. Let's go over.

TEMPLE bumps headlong into a departing customer.

TEMPLE: Oh, I'm so sorry, sir.

MAN: (*Laughing*) That's quite all right.

TEMPLE: You've dropped your paper.

MAN: Oh, thank you!

FADE UP the piano and café chatter for a few moments, then FADE DOWN to the background as SIR GRAHAM and TEMPLE arrive at their table.

FORBES: You sit there, Temple – you can see the door better.

TEMPLE: Yes, all right.

FORBES: Who's that girl over there?

TEMPLE: I don't know. I was just looking at her.

FORBES: She'll certainly know me again! Cigarette?

TEMPLE: Oh, thanks. (*He takes a cigarette*)

FORBES: (*Flicking his lighter*) Do you see any sign of Marx?

TEMPLE: (*Looking about him*) No. He's not here at the moment.

42

FORBES: You'd recognise him all right, I suppose?

TEMPLE: Oh yes, don't worry about that. I'd know Harry Marx anywhere. Ah – here's Worth.

FORBES: Where?

TEMPLE: He's just coming over …

HENRY WORTH is tense and nervous. He is considerably less sure of himself than usual.

WORTH: Good evening, sir.

TEMPLE: Good evening, Mr Worth.

WORTH: Is there anything I can get you, sir?

TEMPLE: Well, we're waiting for a friend of ours, so would you mind if we didn't give you our order until he arrives?

WORTH: But of course not. (*Moving*) Let me get you an ashtray, sir!

FORBES: Thank you.

WORTH puts an ashtray on the table.

WORTH: Er – Mr Temple …

TEMPLE: Yes?

WORTH: I feel I owe you an apology, sir. Last night, when you were here with Mrs Temple, I must have sounded both extremely rude and … very sure of myself.

TEMPLE: Oh, that's all right.

WORTH: I hope you'll accept my apologies, sir.

TEMPLE: There's nothing to apologise about.

WORTH: (*A strange note of panic in his voice*) It's not easy running a café like this, you know, Mr Temple. There are so many restrictions. So much red tape. The police – well – sometimes they are never off my doorstep. I – I try to do the best I can, Mr Temple.

TEMPLE: I'm sure you do.

43

WORTH: (*Tensely, yet anxious to impress*) If you want to know anything about me – about my character, I mean – ask Inspector Perry. He knows me. He knows me personally. He knows I always … try to play the game.

TEMPLE: (*Friendly*) You told me last night that you'd never heard of a man called Dr Belasco. Was that the truth?

WORTH: Yes.

TEMPLE: You know who this gentleman is, don't you?

WORTH: Yes. (*To FORBES*) I recognised you immediately, sir – from your photographs.

FORBES: (*Drily*) Did you? You ought to be on my staff, Mr Worth.

TEMPLE: We have an appointment with a man called Harry Marx. He asked us to meet him here at ten o'clock.

WORTH: Harry Marx?

TEMPLE: Yes. Do you know him?

WORTH: … Yes. Yes, I know him. I don't like him. He's a notorious character. I don't encourage that sort of person to frequent my café.

FORBES: When was the last time you saw Mr Marx?

WORTH: About four weeks ago.

FORBES: Here at the café?

WORTH: Yes. He dropped in one night – about seven o'clock. He stayed for five or ten minutes, that's all.

FORBES: I see.

WORTH: Will you excuse me? I have … rather a lot of things to attend to just at the moment.

TEMPLE: (*Watching WORTH*) Goodbye, Mr Worth.

WORTH: (*Going*) Goodnight, Mr Temple.

A pause.

FORBES: I'm not so sure that Perry's right about that young man.

TEMPLE: Something's happened to him – he's scared. Now I wonder what exactly has scared … Hello, here's that girl we were talking about.

BILLIE CHANDLER arrives at the table. She is an attractive girl of about twenty-eight. A cockney. BILLIE knows all the questions and all the answers.

BILLIE: This seat taken, ducks?

FORBES: Yes, I'm afraid it is.

TEMPLE: (*Interrupting FORBES; pleasantly*) No, I don't think it is. Allow me!

TEMPLE moves a chair for BILLIE.

BILLIE: Oh! Oh, thanks very much! You two boys together?

TEMPLE: You ought to know.

BILLIE: What do you mean?

TEMPLE: You've been watching us for the last five minutes.

BILLIE: Well, I like that, I must say! (*A moment*) Is your name Forbes?

FORBES: Yes.

BILLIE: I've got a message for you.

FORBES: For me?

BILLIE: Yes. From Harry – Harry Marx.

FORBES: What is the message?

BILLIE: (*Suspiciously*) Is he a friend of yours?

FORBES: Yes. It's all right, Miss, em –?

BILLIE: Chandler. Billie Chandler.

FORBES: It's all right, Miss Chandler, you can talk.

A moment.

BILLIE: Harry's waiting for you. He's outside of town.

FORBES: (*Faintly annoyed*) He told me to meet him here at ten o'clock.

45

BILLIE: I know! I know! But he couldn't – he couldn't take any chances.

TEMPLE: Where is he?

BILLIE doesn't answer.

TEMPLE: My name is Temple – Paul Temple.

BILLIE: (*A pause: then:*) He's in a car on the Great North Road. It's parked about six miles this side of Longford.

FORBES: How long should it take us to reach him?

BILLIE: About an hour. Perhaps less, if you step on it.

TEMPLE: (*Quite simply*) We'll step on it.

Play Incidental Music.

CUT TO: TEMPLE's Car.

It is travelling fast.

FORBES: Are we nearly there?

BILLIE: Yes. You'll see the car in a moment.

A pause.

TEMPLE: Is that it?

BILLIE: Yes.

TEMPLE slows the car.

TEMPLE: What do you want me to do?

BILLIE: Stop short – about thirty or forty yards.

TEMPLE: Yes, all right.

FORBES: He's got his lights on … Oh, they're off now.

BILLIE: It's all right, it's only a signal. Pull into the side.

TEMPLE draws the car into the side of the road.

TEMPLE: This all right?

The car stops: the engine is still running.

BILLIE: Yes, that's all right.

FORBES: Well, shall we get out?

BILLIE: No! No, wait here! I'll fetch him. I shan't be long.

FORBES: Why don't we walk across to the car with you? It'll save time.

BILLIE: No, he wants you to wait here.

FORBES: Why? I'm not at all sure that I like the look of this, Miss Chandler.

BILLIE: It's all right! Honest. Honest, it's all right. There's nothing to worry about. Don't you see, Harry's just cautious, he's frightened that –

TEMPLE: He's frightened that someone else might have picked you up and forced you to bring them out here.

BILLIE: Yes.

FORBES: All right. Fetch him.

BILLIE opens the car door and gets out. We hear her footsteps receding on the country road.

TEMPLE: I'll switch the engine off.

TEMPLE does so. There is a slight pause. In the distance we can hear the engine of the other car.

FORBES: Hello …

TEMPLE: He's got his engine running.

FORBES: Yes.

A pause.

TEMPLE: She's nearly reached the car.

FORBES: (*Watching*) Yes.

BILLIE: (*Calling out*) Harry, it's Billie! It's O.K. – he's here!

Then BILLIE gives a quick, startled scream.

FORBES: What is it?

TEMPLE: She's seen something! I've got a hunch that Marx isn't in the – my God!

There is another scream from BILLIE and the sound of machine gun fire from the other car. Simultaneously, the other car revs up and starts to drive towards TEMPLE's.

FORBES: Temple!

47

TEMPLE: They were waiting for us!

FORBES: The car's coming!

TEMPLE: Get down! Get down, Sir Graham!

During the above dialogue the other car has raced down the road and is now almost level with TEMPLE's. There is a sudden, extremely loud burst of machine gunfire. The bullets smash up against TEMPLE's car, bursting the tyres, smashing the windscreen and the windows to pieces. Then the car roars past and away.

TEMPLE: Are you all right? (*Silence*) Sir Graham …? Sir Graham!

FORBES: I – twisted – my leg – getting down – (*Straightening himself*) That's better.

TEMPLE: You're sure?

FORBES: Yes, I'm all right.

TEMPLE opens his door.

TEMPLE: Then come along.

TEMPLE and FORBES get out of the car.

Play Incidental Music.

CUT TO: The Roadside.

PAUL and SIR GRAHAM are by BILLIE's body.

FORBES: Poor kid, she hadn't a chance. She hadn't a dog's chance, Temple.

TEMPLE: Let's carry her back to the car.

FORBES: Yes, all right.

TEMPLE and FORBES pick up BILLIE's body and start to carry her back along the road to TEMPLE's car.

TEMPLE: Can you manage?

FORBES: Yes, I'll manage … What do you think happened?

TEMPLE: It's obvious what happened. Belasco and his crowd discovered what Marx was up to and trailed him here.

FORBES: Do you think they've got Marx in the car then?

TEMPLE: No; it's a thousand to one he's dead – and if you want my opinion he's not far from here.

FORBES: Yes, I shouldn't be surprised.

They've arrived at the car.

TEMPLE: Right – let's put her on the back seat – open the door.

SIR GRAHAM opens the door and they put BILLIE on the back seat.

TEMPLE: There – we – are.

FORBES: Poor kid. She little knew what was in store for her.

TEMPLE: I'll have a scout round, Sir Graham, and see you back here at the car.

FORBES: All right, Temple.

Play Incidental Music.

CUT TO: The Roadside, a little later.

TEMPLE's footsteps are heard on the road as he arrives at the car.

FORBES: Well?

TEMPLE: Marx is dead all right. They dumped him in a ditch about twenty yards from where their car was parked.

FORBES: M'm – well that's that.

TEMPLE: (*Thoughtfully*) I found this wallet on him.

FORBES: They can't have searched him.

TEMPLE: No; we probably arrived on the scene a little sooner than they expected.

FORBES: What's that card you've got?

TEMPLE: M'm? Oh, it was in the wallet – it's an invitation to a party.

FORBES: What sort of party?

TEMPLE: (*Almost dismissing the matter*) Apparently a cocktail party.

FORBES: I shouldn't have thought that Harry Marx was the sort of man who went to cocktail parties!

TEMPLE: No. You wouldn't have thought so.

FORBES: What's it say?

TEMPLE: It says: "You are cordially invited to a cocktail party at 27A Berkeley House Place on Friday, April 4th, at 6.30 pm".

FORBES: April 4th … That's tomorrow.

TEMPLE: Yes.

FORBES: (*Intrigued*) Is it addressed to Harry Marx?

TEMPLE: Yes, it's addressed to Marx all right.

FORBES: (*Faintly exasperated*) Well, who's it from?

TEMPLE: It's from a lady called Mrs Forester.

Play Incidental Music.

The doorbell rings, and then rings again as JOSEPH approaches over the tiled floor and opens the door to TEMPLE.

JOSEPH: Good evening, sir …

JOSEPH is a man of about fifty; he sounds a foreigner although oddly enough he hasn't a definite accent. His voice gives the impression of a calm, imperturbable, somewhat sinister personality.

TEMPLE: Good evening.

TEMPLE enters, JOSEPH shuts the door.

JOSEPH: Shall I take your coat, sir?

TEMPLE: Thank you. I suppose most of the other guests have been here for hours.

JOSEPH: Guests, sir?

TEMPLE: Yes.

JOSEPH: I think there must be some mistake, sir.

TEMPLE: For the cocktail party.

JOSEPH:	We haven't a cocktail party, sir – not today, sir.
TEMPLE:	This *is* 27A – Mrs Forester's?
JOSEPH:	Oh, yes. Yes, indeed, sir.
TEMPLE:	Well, I had an invitation to a cocktail party … Oh, a long time ago. As a matter of fact, I think I've got it here somewhere –
JOSEPH:	The party was cancelled, sir. (*Almost an imitation of TEMPLE*) Oh, a long time ago. Mrs Forester wrote to the guests personally. I'm surprised you didn't receive a letter, sir.
TEMPLE:	Yes, I'm – er – rather surprised myself. (*Going*) Oh well, if the party's off – (*He stops; curious*) By the way, haven't I seen you before somewhere?
JOSEPH:	Not that I'm aware of, sir.
TEMPLE:	I was under the impression that I bumped into you last night at a café in Soho.
JOSEPH:	Why, no, sir.
TEMPLE:	Are you sure?
JOSEPH:	Quite sure, sir.

The lounge door opens.

TEMPLE:	I'm not usually mistaken when – (*He stops*)

MRS FORESTER: What is it, Joseph?

MRS FORESTER has a pleasant, attractive voice.

JOSEPH:	I think it's the gentleman you've been expecting, Madam.

MRS FORESTER: (*Approaching*) Oh, yes! How stupid of me! How do you do, Mr Temple? I'm

51

Mrs Forester. Won't you come into the lounge?

A moment.

TEMPLE: You've been expecting me?

MRS FORESTER: (*Laughing*) But of course!

Closing Music.

END OF EPISODE TWO

EPISODE THREE

PRESENTING ED BELLAMY

OPEN TO:

ANNOUNCER: Paul Temple, the celebrated novelist and private detective, is visited by Sir Graham Forbes of Scotland Yard and by a Mr Philip Kaufman who is attached to the Special Branch. Kaufman tells Paul Temple about a notorious criminal known as Dr Belasco. Temple promises to try and discover the identity of Belasco, and during the course of certain investigations makes the acquaintance of David Nelson and Henry Worth. Worth is the proprietor of a small café in Soho. Late one afternoon, during a conference at Scotland Yard, Sir Graham receives a letter from a man known as Harry Marx, who promises to reveal the identity of Dr Belasco. Marx is murdered however, and Temple discovers, on searching the body, that Marx has received an invitation to a cocktail party from a certain Mrs Forester. The following evening Temple presents himself at 27A Berkeley House Place.

CUT TO: The Hallway of 27A Berkeley House Place.

TEMPLE: This is 27A – Mrs Forester's?

JOSEPH: Oh, yes. Yes, indeed, sir.

TEMPLE: Well, I had an invitation to a cocktail party … Oh, a long time ago. As a matter of fact, I think I've got it here somewhere –

JOSEPH: The party was cancelled, sir. (*Almost an imitation of TEMPLE*) Oh, a long time ago. Mrs Forester wrote to the

	guests personally. I'm surprised you didn't receive a letter, sir.
TEMPLE:	Yes, I'm – er – rather surprised myself. (*Going*) Oh well, if the party's off – (*He stops; curious*) By the way, haven't I seen you before somewhere?
JOSEPH:	Not that I'm aware of, sir.
TEMPLE:	I was under the impression that I bumped into you last night at a café in Soho.
JOSEPH:	Why, no, sir.
TEMPLE:	Are you sure?
JOSEPH:	Quite sure, sir.

The lounge door opens.

| TEMPLE: | I'm not usually mistaken when – (*He stops*) |
| MRS FORESTER: | What is it, Joseph? |

MRS FORESTER has a pleasant, attractive voice.

| JOSEPH: | I think it's the gentleman you've been expecting, Madam. |
| MRS FORESTER: | (*Approaching*) Oh, yes! How stupid of me! How do you do, Mr Temple? I'm Mrs Forester. Won't you come into the lounge? |

A moment.

TEMPLE:	You've been expecting me?
MRS FORESTER:	(*Laughing*) But of course! (*Moving*) Do come into the lounge, Mr Temple. Joseph, we'd like some cocktails.
JOSEPH:	Yes, Madam.

Cross to the lounge: TEMPLE and MRS FORESTER enter.

TEMPLE: I was under the impression that you were having a cocktail party, Mrs Forester.

MRS FORESTER: Yes, I overheard you say so. No, I'm afraid I had to call the party off. It was my intention to present Martinez you know, but –

TEMPLE: Martinez?

MRS FORESTER: The South American pianist.

TEMPLE: Oh, yes.

MRS FORESTER: The poor darling was taken ill on the boat coming over and – well – what with one thing and another the whole thing became rather a bore. Oh, but please, do sit down.

TEMPLE: Mrs Forester …

MRS FORESTER: Yes?

TEMPLE: You know, of course, that I never received an invitation to your party?

MRS FORESTER: (*Quite pleasantly*) Yes, of course.

TEMPLE: And yet, nevertheless, you apparently expected me?

MRS FORESTER: Oh, not to the party, Mr Temple. I just – expected you.

TEMPLE: (*Slowly*) What do you mean?

MRS FORESTER: (*A moment, then:*) As a matter of curiosity, what did David Nelson tell you about me?

TEMPLE: He told me that you were a very close friend of his wife's.

MRS FORESTER: Is that all he told you?

TEMPLE: That's all.

MRS FORESTER: You know, of course, that Rene – his wife – committed suicide?

57

TEMPLE: Yes.

MRS FORESTER: She was a very close friend of mine:
we were very attached to each other. It
was a very great shock to me when I
heard what had happened.

TEMPLE: Yes, I'm sure it must have been.

MRS FORESTER: For some peculiar reason, David got it
into his head that I was mixed up in the
whole business. I don't know quite why
he should think that, but he did.

TEMPLE: You still haven't answered my
question, Mrs Forester – why were you
expecting me?

MRS FORESTER: David employed a private detective – a
girl called Mary Hamilton. He
instructed Miss Hamilton to – well –
pry into my private affairs.

TEMPLE: Well?

MRS FORESTER: Two days ago, Miss Hamilton was
murdered …

TEMPLE: Go on.

MRS FORESTER: Shortly after she was murdered – the
same night in fact – Mr Nelson visited
your flat.

TEMPLE: (*A moment, then:*) What are you
suggesting?

MRS FORESTER: I'm suggesting that David Nelson
commissioned you to investigate his
wife's suicide.

TEMPLE: That I stepped into Miss Hamilton's
shoes.

MRS FORESTER: Yes. And I knew, of course, that it
wouldn't be very long before you took

	it into your head to visit the wicked Mrs Forester.
TEMPLE:	(*Quite simply*) Are you very wicked, Mrs Forester?
MRS FORESTER:	I don't think so.
TEMPLE:	Neither do I. Now if you'd said stupid …
MRS FORESTER:	What do you mean?
TEMPLE:	I came here this evening because I had an invitation: an invitation to your cocktail party. Here it is.

TEMPLE passes over the invitation.

A pause.

MRS FORESTER:	I didn't send you this.
TEMPLE:	No, I know you didn't.
MRS FORESTER:	Then you'd hardly call it an invitation.
TEMPLE:	(*Rather forcefully*) But it is one of your invitation cards?
MRS FORESTER:	Yes. (*A suggestion of tenseness*) Where did you get it from?
TEMPLE:	As a matter of fact, I found it. I found it on the dead body of a man called Harry Marx.
MRS FORESTER:	Harry Marx?
TEMPLE:	Yes.
MRS FORESTER:	But where did he get it from?
TEMPLE:	Didn't you send it to him, Mrs Forester?
MRS FORESTER:	No, I … Of course, I didn't! I've never heard of anyone called Harry Marx!
TEMPLE:	Have you ever heard of anyone called Dr Belasco?
MRS FORESTER:	(*Quietly*) Yes.
TEMPLE:	What do you know about him?

MRS FORESTER:(*Obviously on edge*) I don't know anything about him. I've – I've just heard of him, that's all.

A moment.

TEMPLE: You say Rene Nelson was a friend of yours?

MRS FORESTER:A very close friend.

TEMPLE: Then have you any idea why she committed suicide?

MRS FORESTER:(*Curtly*) No.

TEMPLE: But surely if you were really close friends –

MRS FORESTER:I think you'd better ask Mr Nelson that question!

TEMPLE: Meaning, I presume, that Mr and Mrs Nelson didn't get along too well together?

MRS FORESTER:No, meaning precisely nothing of the sort! So far as I know, they were quite good friends.

TEMPLE: Are you a friend of Mr Nelson's?

MRS FORESTER:No. We see very little of each other.

TEMPLE: You don't like him?

MRS FORESTER:It isn't a question of not liking him. I find him a bore. I don't care for bores, Mr Temple.

TEMPLE: (*Pleasantly*) Neither do I, Mrs Forester.

The door opens. JOSEPH enters with a tray of drinks.

MRS FORESTER:I'm glad to see we have something in common.

JOSEPH: I've mixed the cocktails, Madam.

MRS FORESTER:Oh, thank you, Joseph. Just put them down there.

JOSEPH puts the tray down on a table.

JOSEPH: Is there anything else, Madam?

MRS FORESTER:No, thank you.

JOSEPH: Thank you, Madam.

JOSEPH leaves, closing the door.

MRS FORESTER:(*Quite pleasantly, taking glasses from the tray*) I hope this is to your liking, Mr Temple.

TEMPLE: (*Taking a drink*) Thank you.

MRS FORESTER:Frankly, I'm not a connoisseur of cocktails myself, but my friends tell me Joseph is quite unique at this sort of thing.

TEMPLE: (*Sips*) M'm! How right they are. Delicious.

MRS FORESTER:(*Amused*) I thought you'd like it.

TEMPLE: Next time you really must invite me to your party.

MRS FORESTER:I'll do more than that, Mr Temple, I'll make a point of not cancelling it.

TEMPLE laughs.

TEMPLE: Well – cheers.

MRS FORESTER:Cheers. (*A slight pause; smiling at TEMPLE*) You know, I can't help thinking that you're not exactly a stranger. You see, I've read so many of your books.

TEMPLE: I hope you liked them.

MRS FORESTER:(*Not unpleasantly*) Well, frankly, I didn't. For some unaccountable reason mystery stories always seem to make me laugh. I suppose I must have a perverted sense of humour. Still, I do hope that won't stop us from becoming better acquainted.

TEMPLE: I hope not, Mrs Forester. You must meet my wife.

MRS FORESTER: Oh, yes. Yes, I must.

Play Incidental Music.

CUT TO: The Corridor Outside PAUL and STEVE's Flat.

The lift arrives, the gates open and shut, as PAUL gets out, whistling to himself. He walks to the door of the flat and presses the button. We hear the flat buzzer. TEMPLE continues to hum and whistle to himself. Then he presses the button again.

TEMPLE: Come along, Charlie! Come along!

He presses the button again, and then the door is suddenly thrown open.

TEMPLE: Charlie, I've been standing here for hours – Oh! Hello, Mr Nelson …

NELSON: Oh, it's you! I wasn't sure whether I'd heard the bell or not.

TEMPLE closes the door.

TEMPLE: What's happened? What are you doing here?

NELSON: Well – as a matter of fact, I was just going to mix your wife a drink. I was trying to find the ice.

TEMPLE: (*Watching NELSON*) It's in the kitchen – surprisingly enough in the refrigerator.

NELSON: Oh … (*A little laugh*) Oh!

STEVE: (*Calling from the lounge*) Is that you, darling?

TEMPLE: (*Calling back*) Yes! What's going on here, Steve?

NELSON: I'm afraid we had rather a nasty accident this
afternoon, Mr Temple – your wife's pretty
badly shaken.

TEMPLE: Is she all right?

NELSON: Yes, yes, she's all right, but – well – you know
– it's … it's nerves.

TEMPLE moves into the lounge.

TEMPLE: Hello, Steve – what's the matter?

STEVE: Hello, Paul …

TEMPLE: Don't get up, darling. What's happened?

STEVE: I was out shopping and bumped into Mr
Nelson. He said that he wanted to have a chat
to you and suggested that – (*She winces*)

TEMPLE: What is it? Are you in pain?

STEVE: No, I – I just feel jumpy, that's all.

NELSON arrives with an iced drink for STEVE.

NELSON: Here we are, Mrs Temple. Drink this.

STEVE: Oh, thank you.

STEVE takes the glass and drinks.

NELSON: Drink it up!

STEVE finishes the drink.

STEVE: Phew! What was in that – dynamite?

NELSON: That little concoction is known as the Nelson
Knockout!

STEVE: You're telling me.

TEMPLE: Do you feel better?

STEVE: Much better.

TEMPLE: Good.

NELSON: I am awfully sorry about this, Mr Temple.

TEMPLE: But what happened?

NELSON: Well – I'd been trying to make up my mind to
telephone you all day. I was rather worried
about something, and I felt that if we could
have a chat together you might possibly be able

to straighten things out for me. You see, since I last saw you, something has happened: something which I feel so far as the Belasco affair is concerned – is rather   important …

TEMPLE: Go on, Mr Nelson.

NELSON: (*Suddenly: almost interrupting his own thoughts*) Anyway, to get back to my story. About a quarter past four this afternoon, I strolled into the book department at Dolmans. I bought a novel and was getting my change from the assistant when suddenly, to my surprise (*Start music*) I noticed Mrs Temple staring at me across the counter. To be perfectly frank with you, it took me two or three seconds before I actually recognised her …

FADE UP MUSIC then mix into:

CUT TO: Dolmans Bookshop.

STEVE: (*Pleasantly*) Hello, Mr Nelson!

NELSON: Why, Mrs Temple! Do forgive me! I'm afraid I didn't recognise you! How are you?

STEVE: I'm quite well, thank you.

NELSON: And Mr Temple?

STEVE: He's fine.

NELSON: He's not with you at the moment, I take it?

STEVE: No, I'm afraid not. As a matter of fact, he's getting ready to go to a cocktail party.

NELSON: (*Laughing*) Oh, I see … Will he be in later this evening?

STEVE: Yes, I think so.

NELSON: (*Hesitantly*) I rather wanted to have a talk with him some time, I don't know whether it would be   convenient to come round –

64

STEVE: Why don't you call round tonight – about nine
            o'clock – he's almost bound to be in then.
NELSON: May I?
STEVE: Yes, of course.
NELSON: Thank you.
STEVE: Is there any message I can give him?
NELSON: No, I … (*Suddenly: a complete change*) Yes!
            Yes, you can tell him, that I … know now why
            my wife committed suicide.
STEVE: Yes, all right, Mr Nelson, I'll tell him that.
NELSON: (*Brighter*) Can I give you a lift anywhere, Mrs
            Temple?
STEVE: Well …
NELSON: It was raining heavily a few minutes ago, I
            don't know whether it still is or not.
STEVE: Well, actually I'm going back to the flat –
NELSON: Oh, splendid! That's easy –
STEVE: I don't want to take you out of your way, Mr
            Nelson.
NELSON: You're not, I assure you. Here, let me give you
            a hand with those parcels! Oh! I see you've
            bought a copy of "Forever".
STEVE: That's for Charlie! It's his birthday on
            Tuesday, and – well – you know the servant
            problem.
NELSON: Yes. Yes, rather.

CUT TO: The Busy Street Outside the Bookshop.
*We hear the sounds of traffic and passers-by. There is very
heavy rain. STEVE and NELSON approach his car.*
STEVE: What weather! Isn't it dreadful!
NELSON: Allow me.
NELSON opens the passenger door for STEVE.
STEVE: Thank you!

STEVE gets in with her parcels.

STEVE: I'm very glad I … oh, I bumped into you, Mr Nelson!

NELSON: I certainly don't think you'd have picked up a taxi very easily!

STEVE: I'm quite certain I shouldn't!

CUT TO: Inside NELSON's Car.

The car is travelling at a medium speed.

STEVE: I don't think it's raining quite so heavily.

NELSON: No, perhaps not. What time did you say, Mrs Temple? Nine o'clock?

STEVE: Yes, drop in about nine – Paul's almost sure to be back by then.

NELSON: Good. (*His eyes on the road*) It's awfully skiddy. (*After a moment*) Mrs Temple …

STEVE: Yes?

NELSON: You remember me telling you about a woman called Mrs Forester.

STEVE: Yes?

NELSON: Well, I've got a shrewd suspicion that I was right.

STEVE: What do you mean?

NELSON: (*After a pause: thoughtfully*) I've been watching her – or rather, I've been watching her house. A young man called to see her last night. It was very late – almost twelve o'clock. When he left the house I, eh … I followed him.

STEVE: Well?

NELSON: I discovered who he was. It's the man your husband mentioned. His name's Worth.

STEVE: Worth! Are you sure it was Mr Worth?

NELSON: Yes, quite sure. I followed him back to the café.

STEVE:	But why should Mr Worth visit – (*Suddenly alarmed*) What is it? Are we skidding or … What is it?
NELSON:	I don't know! I … I don't know! There seems to be something the matter with the … the steering – It won't – it won't pull the wheels towards –
STEVE:	Do something or we shall be on the pavement!
NELSON:	I can't stop it! It's no use, I –
STEVE:	Where's the handbrake? Oh, for heaven's sake be quick! Be quick, Mr Nelson!

There is a crash as the car rides the pavement, a screeching of brakes, and a volley of sound as the car strikes a lamp-standard.

CUT TO: The Street, by the crashed car, a few seconds later.

We hear the excited voices of passers-by.

NELSON:	Mrs Temple – are you all right?
STEVE:	(*Weakly*) Yes, I … I …
NELSON:	Are you sure? Are you sure you're all right?
STEVE:	Yes … Can I get out of the car, I …
NELSON:	Yes, yes of course! I'm sorry! Give me your hand! …

STEVE climbs out of the car.

NELSON:	Watch … watch your coat; don't tear it on the glass.
STEVE:	Are you all right yourself?
NELSON:	Yes. Ye Gods, we were lucky!
STEVE:	What happened? Was it a skid?

NELSON: No, I don't think it was. It seemed to me
             as if the steering went to pieces – I just
             couldn't do anything with it.

BELLAMY: It certainly wasn't a skid – I can tell you
             that right now!

ED BELLAMY is a man of about thirty-five: he has a
tough, yet not exactly common personality. He speaks with
a slight American accent.

NELSON: No, I don't think it was.

BELLAMY: I saw the whole thing – I was parked on
             the other side of the road. Gee, I wondered
             what was going to happen next! One
             minute you were blissfully sailing along as
             if (*He stops: quietly*) Say, are you feeling
             queer?

STEVE: I'm feeling a little dizzy.

The sound of an approaching police car is heard.

BELLAMY: You'd better relax. Come along, I'll take
             you over to my car.

STEVE: That's awfully nice of you, but I think I'll
             be all right if I just … just …

NELSON: No, no, you go along! Please. There's a lot
             I've got to attend to. I'll be over in a few
             minutes.

BELLAMY: That's my car over on the corner – the
             Rolls. We'll be waiting for you over there.
             O.K.?

NELSON: Thank you very much, sir.

BELLAMY: You're welcome! By the way, were you
             going far?

NELSON: No, I was simply running this lady home –
             to Half Moon Street.

BELLAMY: Well, we'll soon take care of that! Let us
             know when you're ready.

NELSON: (*Going*) Thanks.

CUT TO: The TEMPLES' Flat. The Lounge. As Before.
TEMPLE: Yes. (*A moment*) Were you surprised, Mr
              Nelson, when you found out what had
              happened?

A pause.

NELSON: No.
TEMPLE: Why not?
NELSON: Because … Before I answer that question,
              Temple, would you mind telling me
              something?
TEMPLE: That rather depends what it is.
NELSON: Do I strike you as being a rather frightened
              sort of person?
TEMPLE: The first time I met you – or rather, when I
              met you at the Villa-Rica – I got the
              impression that you were a particularly
              self-possessed sort of person. Now,
              however, I'm not so sure. Still, you don't
              exactly strike me as being frightened of
              anything. Nervous, perhaps – but not
              exactly frightened, Mr Nelson.
NELSON: Well, I am frightened. What happened this
              afternoon with Mrs Temple has happened
              before. It's not the first time.
STEVE: What do you mean?
NELSON: I mean it's not the first time there's been
              an attempt on my life. That's why I
              wanted to get in touch with you.
TEMPLE: Go on, Mr Nelson.
NELSON: After what you told me about Mary
              Hamilton, I made up my mind to make
              certain investigations myself.

69

TEMPLE: Investigations about what, exactly?

NELSON: I told you. I wanted to find out why my wife committed suicide. That's why I engaged Mary Hamilton.

TEMPLE: Did you find out why your wife committed suicide?

NELSON: (*A little surprised by TEMPLE's manner*) Yes.

TEMPLE: Well?

NELSON: Apparently, Rene borrowed some money from Mrs Forester. She was unable to repay that money and after a little while Mrs Forester became rather – well – rather difficult about it.

TEMPLE: How do you know this?

NELSON: I found some letters: some letters belonging to my wife.

TEMPLE: From Mrs Forester?

NELSON: (*Hesitantly*) Yes.

TEMPLE: You told Mrs Temple that Mr Worth visited Mrs Forester's – are you sure of that?

NELSON: Quite sure. I followed him back to the café.

TEMPLE: Was he alone?

NELSON: Yes.

TEMPLE: Nelson: are you under the impression that your wife didn't commit suicide?

NELSON: What do you mean?

TEMPLE: Do you think she was murdered?

NELSON: No. The coroner brought in a verdict of suicide and I'm quite prepared to accept that verdict. What I'm not prepared to accept, however, is the general assumption that we were all washed up and that our marriage was on the rocks.

TEMPLE: In other words, you don't wish to –

The telephone starts to ring.

TEMPLE: Excuse me.

TEMPLE lifts the receiver.

TEMPLE: (*On the phone*) Hello?

FORBES: (*On the other end of the phone*) Hello? Temple?

TEMPLE: Speaking.

FORBES: Forbes here.

TEMPLE: Oh, hello, Sir Graham.

FORBES: How did you get on this evening?

TEMPLE: (*Hesitantly*) Oh, you mean – at – the cocktail   party?

FORBES: Yes – Mrs Forester's. Did you see her?

TEMPLE: Yes, but it wasn't quite what we expected.

FORBES: Oh. In what way?

TEMPLE: Well, eh …

FORBES: Aren't you alone?

TEMPLE: Not just at the moment.

FORBES: Oh, I see. I'll ring later.

TEMPLE: Well – as a matter of fact, Sir Graham, I rather wanted to see you.

FORBES: Tonight?

TEMPLE: No, tomorrow morning will do.

FORBES: All right – my office – 10.30. Is that all right?

TEMPLE: Yes, that'll do fine. Oh, and do you think you could arrange for Mr Worth to be there?

FORBES: (*Rather surprised*) Mr Worth? Yes, I think so. I could probably get Inspector Perry to

	pick him up. (*Curious*) Is it urgent, Temple?
TEMPLE:	I'd like to see him, Sir Graham.
FORBES:	All right – he'll be here. 10.30.
TEMPLE:	10.30.

TEMPLE replaces the receiver.

A slight pause.

NELSON:	Temple?
TEMPLE:	Yes?
NELSON:	Why do you think Worth went to Mrs Forester's?
TEMPLE:	He might be a friend of hers.
NELSON:	It seems rather a curious coincidence, doesn't it?
TEMPLE:	What do you mean?
NELSON:	Well, first of all you heard about him from Ross Morgan, an associate of Dr Belasco's, then you discovered that Mary Hamilton was working at his café, and now apparently, he turns out to be a friend of Mrs Forester's.
STEVE:	It is rather a remarkable coincidence, darling.
TEMPLE:	Do you think so?
NELSON:	Don't you?
TEMPLE:	(*Thoughtfully*) Yes, I suppose it is.

Play Incidental Music.

CUT TO: SIR GRAHAM's Office, Scotland Yard.

PHILIP KAUFMAN's manner is irritable, and he is faintly aggressive.

KAUFMAN:	…Well, if you'll pardon my saying so, Mr Temple, it seems to me that your visit to Mrs Forester's was something of a fiasco!

You went there with the intention of finding out why exactly Harry Marx received an invitation to her cocktail party, and yet apparently you hesitated to ask her the question point-blank –

TEMPLE: I did ask her the question point-blank, Mr Kaufman, and she gave me a point-blank answer!

FORBES: (*Trying to ease the situation*) In fact, she said quite frankly that she'd never heard of Harry Marx.

TEMPLE: Exactly.

KAUFMAN: But it's nonsense. She must have heard of Marx! Did you speak to her about the other girl – the one that committed suicide?

TEMPLE: Yes.

KAUFMAN: What did she say?

TEMPLE: Well, she confirmed what Mr Nelson had already told me.

KAUFMAN: Did she tell you that Mrs Nelson had borrowed money from her?

TEMPLE: No.

KAUFMAN: Did you ask her if she had?

TEMPLE: (*Irritated*) Of course I didn't ask her.

KAUFMAN: No?

TEMPLE: No!

KAUFMAN: You surprise me, Mr Temple!

FORBES: Temple knew nothing about the money or the letters from Mrs Forester until he saw Nelson, and he didn't see Nelson until he returned to the flat –

There is a knock on the door and INSPECTOR PERRY enters.

FORBES:	What is it?
PERRY:	I beg your pardon, sir, but …
FORBES:	Oh, come in, Inspector.
PERRY:	Oh, good morning, Mr Temple.
TEMPLE:	Good morning, Inspector.
PERRY:	Mr Worth is here, sir.
FORBES:	Oh – ask him in.
PERRY:	If you'll excuse me mentioning it, sir, I think I'd go a bit easy on the boy. When I picked him up this morning, he got quite panicky, sir.
FORBES:	Perhaps it was the thought of coming to Scotland Yard.
PERRY:	It might have been, sir.
FORBES:	All right, Inspector – ask him in.

PERRY returns to the door.

PERRY:	Come this way, Mr Worth.
WORTH:	Thank you.

PERRY leaves, closing the door.

FORBES:	(*Pleasantly*) Good morning!
WORTH:	Good morning, Sir Graham. (*Surprised*) Oh, good morning, Mr Temple!
TEMPLE:	Good morning.
FORBES:	Do sit down, please.
WORTH:	Thank you. (*He sits*) Inspector Perry told me that you wanted to ask me a few questions, although for the life of me I can't imagine why you should take the trouble to drag me along –
TEMPLE:	Mr Worth.
WORTH:	Yes, Mr Temple?
TEMPLE:	Do you know a lady called Mrs Forester?
WORTH:	Mrs Forester?
TEMPLE:	Yes.

WORTH:	I'm afraid I don't.
TEMPLE:	Her address is 27A Berkeley House Place.
WORTH:	Well?
TEMPLE:	Didn't you visit that address, quite recently in fact?
WORTH:	(*Surprised*) No.
TEMPLE:	You're sure?
WORTH:	Of course I'm sure!
KAUFMAN:	That's a lie!
WORTH:	What do you mean? Who is this man?
KAUFMAN:	My name is Kaufman.
FORBES:	Mr Kaufman is attached to the Special Branch.
WORTH:	Well, Mr Kaufman, for your information I am not in the habit of telling lies.
TEMPLE:	You didn't visit 27A Berkeley House Place?
WORTH:	I did not!
TEMPLE:	Mr Worth, tell me; did you know that Mary Hamilton was a private enquiry agent?
WORTH:	Not until Inspector Perry told me.
FORBES:	And yet Mary Hamilton was employed at your café as a waitress!
WORTH:	I have several waitresses employed at my café, Sir Graham, but they are not – so far as I know – private enquiry agents.
TEMPLE:	You know what happened the other night, I suppose, the night Sir Graham and I visited your café?
WORTH:	Yes.
TEMPLE:	A man called Harry Marx was murdered.
WORTH:	I know that.
TEMPLE:	Do you know why he was murdered?

75

WORTH:	No.
TEMPLE:	He was murdered because he was on the point of divulging the identity of Dr Belasco!
WORTH:	Well?
TEMPLE:	You told us that Harry Marx frequently visited your café.
WORTH:	I did not! I told you that he came to the café – well – occasionally.
TEMPLE:	Did you murder Harry Marx, Mr Worth?
WORTH:	You come to my café – where I am trying my damnedest to carry on a perfectly honest and legitimate business – and you pester me day and night with questions. I have never heard of your precious Mrs Forester. I don't know <u>who</u> Dr Belasco is. I can't imagine <u>why</u> Mary Hamilton was working at my café, and I did not murder Harry Marx!
TEMPLE:	(*Quietly*) Who did?

A pause.

WORTH:	If you want to know about Harry Marx, why don't you ask Mr Bellamy?
TEMPLE:	Mr Bellamy? Who's Mr Bellamy?
FORBES:	Do you mean Ed Bellamy, the man that runs the Machicha Club?
WORTH:	Yes.
FORBES:	Was he a friend of Marx's?
WORTH:	According to what I have heard Marx bought an interest in the club.
FORBES:	When?
WORTH:	Oh, a little while ago.
KAUFMAN:	Where is the Machicha Club?
WORTH:	It's in Berkeley Square.

TEMPLE: Oh, yes. Yes, I know the place. It's a sort of South American set-up. The waiters are dressed as Gauchos.

FORBES: That's it! That's the place!

TEMPLE: M'm. So it's owned by a man called Bellamy?

Play Incidental Music.

CUT TO: The Machicha Club

A dance orchestra are playing a gay South American dance tune. There is background noise of a crowded restaurant.

WAITER: (*A foreigner: suave*) Will you come this way, please, sir – Madam?

TEMPLE: Thank you.

STEVE: (*Crossing the place with TEMPLE*) I rather like the look of this place, darling!

TEMPLE: Certainly looks very gay.

They walk on and arrive at their table.

WAITER: Here we are, Madam. I'm afraid this is the only table I can offer you, sir.

TEMPLE: That's all right.

WAITER: Your waiter will be along in a few moments.

TEMPLE: Thank you. Oh - is Mr Bellamy available?

WAITER: Mr Bellamy? I think he's in his office, sir.

TEMPLE: Well, would you be kind enough to ask him if he could spare me a few moments? My name is Temple.

WAITER: Mr Temple?

TEMPLE: Yes.

WAITER: (*Going*) Very good, sir.

STEVE: Do you think it is the same man, Paul?

TEMPLE: I should imagine it must be; it's the same
            name. What was he like, darling – the man
            who drove you back to the flat?
STEVE: Oh – he was about thirty-six or seven.
            Very smartly dressed, slight American
            accent. Tough, I suppose, in rather a
            pleasant sort of way.
TEMPLE: Glasses?
STEVE: Yes, he wore those square looking glasses,
            you know the sort I mean.
TEMPLE: M'm.
STEVE: If it is the same man, I take it he's got
            quite a reputation?
TEMPLE: Yes, he's supposed to be a pretty smart
            customer.
STEVE: Here's the waiter.
WAITER: Mr Bellamy will see you, sir.
TEMPLE: Thank you.
WAITER: The office is on the second floor, sir.
TEMPLE: I'll find it. I shan't be long, darling.
STEVE: All right.
FADE DOWN the dance orchestra: slow, gradual FADE.

CUT TO: BELLAMY's Office.
*The orchestra is now a very distant background sound. A
knock is heard, and the door opens.*
TEMPLE: Mr Bellamy?
BELLAMY: That's right! Come in, Mr Temple!
TEMPLE enters, shuts the door.
TEMPLE: I hope I'm not intruding?
BELLAMY: Not at all. As a matter of fact, I had a
            hunch that we'd get together sooner or
            later.

TEMPLE:	My wife tells me that you went out of your way yesterday afternoon to be particularly nice to her. I'm very grateful.
BELLAMY:	It wasn't difficult: she's that kind of person.
TEMPLE:	You actually saw the accident, I take it?
BELLAMY:	Yeah. They were pretty lucky. At one time I really thought they'd bought it. (*Pleasantly*) But I'm quite sure that you didn't drop in on me to talk about the accident.
TEMPLE:	Well, no, as a matter of fact I wanted to ask you a few questions.
BELLAMY:	About Harry Marx?
TEMPLE:	Yes.
BELLAMY:	That's what I thought.
TEMPLE:	Marx is dead. He was murdered – I suppose you know that?
BELLAMY:	Sure – it's in the papers.
TEMPLE:	Was Marx a business associate of yours?
BELLAMY:	Kind of. He bought himself an interest in this place just before Christmas.
TEMPLE:	How much did that cost him?
BELLAMY:	(*A moment's hesitation*) Twelve thousand pounds.
TEMPLE:	Twelve thousand pounds! That's a lot of money.
BELLAMY:	It ain't hay!
A slight pause.	
TEMPLE:	Mr Bellamy?
BELLAMY:	Yes?
TEMPLE:	Who do you think murdered Harry Marx?

BELLAMY:	You're the detective around here! Who do you think murdered him, that's more to the point?
TEMPLE:	(*Watching BELLAMY*) I think he was murdered by a man called Belasco – Dr Belasco.
BELLAMY:	(*Surprised*) Dr Belasco?
TEMPLE:	Yes. The name isn't entirely unfamiliar to you, I take it?
BELLAMY:	Well, not entirely. You're the second guy that's mentioned it to me tonight.
TEMPLE:	Oh? Who was the first?
BELLAMY:	A fellow in the restaurant. He asked me to have a drink with him.
TEMPLE:	What was he like?
BELLAMY:	I'll point him out to you. Turn that table over.
TEMPLE:	What?
BELLAMY:	Turn that table over.

TEMPLE moves the top of the nearby table.

TEMPLE:	By Timothy … It's a periscope.
BELLAMY:	Yeah! I like to see what's going on around here. Look! There's Mrs Temple …
TEMPLE:	(*Laughing*) Yes, I'm just watching her.
BELLAMY:	Now let's turn it around and see if we can find that guy …

BELLAMY moves the periscope round.

TEMPLE:	Do you see him?
BELLAMY:	No, it rather looks to me as if … (*Suddenly*) There he is!
TEMPLE:	Where?
BELLAMY:	Sat over in the corner, near the staircase – do you see him?
TEMPLE:	Yes. Yes, I see him all right.

BELLAMY: Who is he?
TEMPLE: His name's Joseph. He works for a woman
called Mrs Forester.

Closing Music.

END OF EPISODE THREE

EPISODE FOUR

MRS FORESTER IS SURPRISED

OPEN TO:

ANNOUNCER: Paul Temple, the celebrated novelist and private detective, is visited by Sir Graham Forbes of Scotland Yard and by a Mr Philip Kaufman who is attached to the Special Branch. Kaufman tells Paul Temple about a notorious criminal known as Dr Belasco. Temple promises to try and discover the identity of Belasco and during the course of his investigations makes the acquaintance of David Nelson, Henry Worth and a certain Mrs Forester. Worth is the proprietor of a small café in Soho. One afternoon, Sir Graham receives a letter from a man known as Harry Marx. Marx promises to reveal the identity of Dr Belasco but is unfortunately murdered. A little while later, Temple and Steve visit a nightclub owned by a man known as Ed Bellamy. Bellamy is known to have been an associate of Harry Marx. Temple visits Bellamy (*Start Fade*) in his private office …

CUT TO: BELLAMY's Office in the Machicha Club.
The orchestra is very distant background sound.

TEMPLE: Was Marx a business associate of yours?

BELLAMY: Kind of. He bought himself an interest in this place just before Christmas.

TEMPLE: How much did that cost him?

BELLAMY:	(*A moment's hesitation*) Twelve thousand pounds.
TEMPLE:	Twelve thousand pounds! That's a lot of money.
BELLAMY:	It ain't hay!

A slight pause.

TEMPLE:	Mr Bellamy?
BELLAMY:	Yes?
TEMPLE:	Who do you think murdered Harry Marx?
BELLAMY:	You're the detective around here! Who do you think murdered him, that's more to the point?
TEMPLE:	(*Watching BELLAMY*) I think he was murdered by a man called Belasco – Dr Belasco.
BELLAMY:	(*Surprised*) Dr Belasco?
TEMPLE:	Yes. The name isn't entirely unfamiliar to you, I take it?
BELLAMY:	Well, not entirely. You're the second guy that's mentioned it to me tonight.
TEMPLE:	Oh? Who was the first?
BELLAMY:	A fellow in the restaurant. He asked me to have a drink with him.
TEMPLE:	What was he like?
BELLAMY:	I'll point him out to you. Turn that table over.
TEMPLE:	(*Surprised*) What?
BELLAMY:	Turn that table over.

TEMPLE moves the top of the nearby table.

TEMPLE:	By Jove what's this – your own television system?
BELLAMY:	No – a periscope. I like to see what's going on around here. Look! There's Mrs Temple …

TEMPLE: (*Laughing*) Yes, I'm just watching her.

BELLAMY: Now let's turn it around and see if we can find that guy …

BELLAMY moves the periscope round.

TEMPLE: Do you see him?

BELLAMY: No, it rather looks to me as if … (*Suddenly*) There he is!

TEMPLE: Where?

BELLAMY: Sat over in the corner, near the staircase – do you see him?

TEMPLE: Yes. Yes, I see him all right.

BELLAMY: Who is he?

TEMPLE: His name's Joseph. He works for a woman called Mrs Forester. (*A moment*) What exactly did he say to you, Mr Bellamy?

BELLAMY: Well, he just asked me to have a drink with him. I didn't like to offend the guy, so I had a drink.

TEMPLE: How did he come to mention Dr Belasco?

BELLAMY: He suddenly asked me if I knew him. He said it in rather a peculiar way though, as if there was a kind of catch in it. Say, who is this Dr Belasco, anyway?

TEMPLE: (*Watching BELLAMY*) Don't you know?

BELLAMY: If I knew I wouldn't be asking you!

TEMPLE: Well, for some time now there have been a number of small cliques – call them gangs, if you like, in the West End of London. Dr Belasco is determined to coordinate those cliques into one body, one definite organisation.

BELLAMY: With Belasco as the great White Chief, I take it?

TEMPLE: Exactly.

BELLAMY:	He's got some hopes!
TEMPLE:	He's got more than hopes, Mr Bellamy.
BELLAMY:	What do you mean?
TEMPLE:	Well, there are signs – very definite signs in fact – that Belasco is succeeding. This afternoon I had a long confidential chat to Inspector Perry, who is in charge of the investigation.
BELLAMY:	I know Perry. He walks in here as if he had a season ticket.
TEMPLE:	(*Laughing*) Yes, well what Perry doesn't know about the West End is nobody's business! He told me that the protection racket – which hardly existed in this country six months ago – is now carefully planned and efficiently organised. And it isn't only the protection racket either, Mr Bellamy.
BELLAMY:	What do you mean?
TEMPLE:	Four weeks ago, a diamond necklace was stolen. It was valued at approximately a quarter of a million.
BELLAMY:	I know. The Duchess of Harborough's. It was in the papers.
TEMPLE:	Do you know who stole the necklace?
BELLAMY:	(*A moment*) Yeah. There's only one man who could steal it, you know that as well as I do. Larry Bristol. He must have been crazy.
TEMPLE:	Why?
BELLAMY:	Because he'll never get rid of a necklace like that, not in a thousand years.
TEMPLE:	That's just the point!
BELLAMY:	I don't get you.

TEMPLE: Six months ago, Larry Bristol wouldn't have attempted a job like that. But someone quite obviously persuaded him that the necklace could be got rid of. Someone, in fact, carefully organised the whole business.

BELLAMY: Have they picked up Larry?

TEMPLE: Perry picked him up in Liverpool three weeks ago.

BELLAMY: Had he the necklace?

TEMPLE: No, but he had a very satisfactory alibi.

BELLAMY: (*Faintly amused*) This Dr Belasco seems to know all the answers. But why are you telling me all this, Mr Temple? It makes interesting conversation but where does it get us?

TEMPLE: Harry Marx wrote Sir Graham Forbes a letter saying that he knew the identity of Dr Belasco. Shortly after he wrote that letter he was murdered.

BELLAMY: Yeah. And to my way of thinking he asked for it. I never liked Marx. I took his dough because I needed it, but I never liked the guy. Look here, you don't really think that I murdered Marx – that I'm Dr Belasco?

TEMPLE: Are you?

BELLAMY: Sure! I'm also Betty Grable and Monty Woolley! (*Temple laughs*) No, but seriously, just because I knew Harry Marx, you don't really think that I'm mixed up in this business?

TEMPLE: How well did you know him?

BELLAMY: Marx? Pretty well. You see the position, so far as I was concerned, was simply this.

89

Just before Christmas, I struck a pretty bad patch with this place. I needed money. Marx used to come here pretty often. He was a rough diamond but he kind of liked what he called the 'classy set-ups'. One night, he discovered that financially, I was in hot water, and he made me a proposition.

TEMPLE: Did he interfere with you at all?

BELLAMY: What do you mean?

TEMPLE: With the running of this place?

BELLAMY: No … No, he was pretty nice about all that.

TEMPLE: Marx was friendly with a girl called Billie Chandler: did you meet her?

BELLAMY: Why, yes! I knew Billie; she was a nice girl. That was too bad; about what happened, I mean …

TEMPLE: Yes …

BELLAMY: Well, if you'll excuse me, I'll be making a move. It's nice to have met you, Mr Temple! Give my regards to the little lady!

TEMPLE: Thank you.

BELLAMY opens a door.

BELLAMY: Oh, this way, Mr Temple, you'll find it much quicker.

With the opening of the door, we hear more clearly the sound of the club and the dance orchestra.

Play Incidental Music.

CUT TO: The Machicha Club.

The dance music ends. There is applause.

TEMPLE: Hello, Steve.

STEVE: Oh, hello, darling.

TEMPLE: (*Sitting down*) Sorry to have been so long.

STEVE: That's all right. Did you see Mr Bellamy?

TEMPLE: Yes, I saw him. It's your friend all right – he sends his regards.

STEVE: Somehow, I had a feeling it might be. It's rather odd though, isn't it?

TEMPLE: What do you mean?

STEVE: Well, it's rather odd that he should be mixed up in this business, and yet turn up just when Mr Nelson and I had the accident.

TEMPLE: Well, according to Mr Bellamy he's not mixed up in this business.

STEVE: He was a friend of Harry Marx!

The orchestra strikes up a new dance tune.

TEMPLE: Yes, but I'm not sure whether that proves anything or not.

A pause.

STEVE: Paul …

TEMPLE: Yes …

STEVE: When Mr Kaufman first told us about Dr Belasco, he told us that Belasco was starting to form the nucleus of a new organisation.

TEMPLE: Well?

STEVE: Do you think that's true? I mean, for weeks now there's been nothing about Belasco in the newspapers.

TEMPLE: It's true enough; and it's my firm belief that Kaufman didn't exaggerate. (*He stops. Pleasantly, raising his voice*) Good evening!

JOSEPH: (*Taken by surprise*) Oh … good evening, sir.

TEMPLE: I didn't expect to find you here, Joseph.

JOSEPH: No, sir.

TEMPLE: What is this, business or pleasure?

JOSEPH: Purely pleasure, sir – it's my evening off.

TEMPLE:	Oh, I see! I can understand now why you make such excellent cocktails. Obviously, you believe in getting your experience at first hand.
JOSEPH:	Yes, sir.
TEMPLE:	Oh, this is my wife, Joseph.
JOSEPH:	Good evening, Madam.
STEVE:	Good evening.
JOSEPH:	(*Faintly ill at ease*) Will you excuse me, sir?
TEMPLE:	Yes, of course. Give my regards to Mrs Forester.
JOSEPH:	Yes. Yes, I will indeed, sir.

Pause.

STEVE:	Who on earth is that extraordinary individual?
TEMPLE:	His name's Joseph. He works for Mrs Forester.
STEVE:	What do you mean – works for her?
TEMPLE:	Well, the day I arrived he opened the door. I think he's a sort of general factotum.
STEVE:	It's rather strange to find him in this sort of place.
TEMPLE:	That's what I thought.
STEVE:	Did you know he was here?
TEMPLE:	(*Thoughtfully*) Yes, Bellamy pointed him out to me and apparently, he spoke to Bellamy earlier this evening.
STEVE:	What about – do you know?
TEMPLE:	Yes, he asked him if he'd heard of – (*He stops*)
STEVE:	What is it?
TEMPLE:	Who's this?

LORD CRAYMORE arrives: he has a faintly patronising manner.

CRAYMORE: Mr Temple?

TEMPLE: Yes?

CRAYMORE: May I introduce myself. My name's Craymore – Lord Craymore.

TEMPLE: Well … how do you do?

CRAYMORE: I read a book of yours – a long time ago – something to do with a murder or something – couldn't make head or tail of it – always meant to ask you about it.

TEMPLE: What was it called?

CRAYMORE: Ah, now you've got me! Deuce of a long time ago … Fellow pushes girl off a cliff – or knocks her under a train or something. Whole thing was rather far-fetched, I thought.

STEVE: I trust you didn't buy a copy.

CRAYMORE: Oh, no, no, rather not! Borrowed it from a friend. As a matter of fact, Temple, I've – I've got rather a good idea for a detective novel myself. Perhaps we might get together some time?

TEMPLE: Yes, we might.

CRAYMORE: Well, why not later tonight – at your flat?

TEMPLE: Well, I …

CRAYMORE: I could tell you the whole idea and then – (*Lowering his voice*) – perhaps we could talk about … Dr Belasco.

TEMPLE: What do you know about Dr Belasco?

CRAYMORE: Later! At your flat.

TEMPLE: All right.

CRAYMORE: Just after twelve.

TEMPLE: (*Nodding*) We'll be waiting.

Play Incidental Music.

CUT TO: The Machicha Club Entrance Hall. Later.
In the background the orchestra is now playing a slow waltz.
TEMPLE: Ready, Steve?
STEVE: Yes.
TEMPLE: It's a pity we haven't got the car!
STEVE: (*Laughing*) I knew you'd say that!
They pass through the club's swing door, into:

CUT TO: The Street Outside The club.
There is the sound of light traffic and passers-by.
TEMPLE: (*To DOORMAN*) Can you get us a cab?
DOORMAN: I very much doubt it, sir!
STEVE: It's all right, darling, we can walk.
TEMPLE: Walk!
DOORMAN: I haven't seen a taxi for the last half-hour, sir. But if you like to hold on a bit, I'll pop down to the end of the square.
The sound of an approaching taxi.
DOORMAN: Blimey, you are lucky! Taxi! Taxi! (*Aside*) It's o.k., his flag's up.
The taxi slows down and draws into the side.
STEVE: That's a piece of luck.
DOORMAN: It certainly is, Ma'am. (*Apparently surprised as PAUL tips him*) Oh, thank you, sir! (*He opens the taxi door*) Here you are, Ma'am.
STEVE: Oh, thank you.
DOORMAN: Where to, sir?
TEMPLE: Tell him to drop us off at – hello …
STEVE: What is it, Paul?
TEMPLE: Have you seen my gloves?

STEVE: You had them a moment ago.

TEMPLE: Are you sure? (*Searching*) That's funny.

DOORMAN: You don't appear to have dropped them, sir.

DRIVER: Look in your pockets, mate!

TEMPLE: No ... I ... Are you sure I had them, darling?

STEVE: Yes, I think so.

TEMPLE: I know what's happened, I've left them in the cloakroom. (*Going*) Hold on a moment – I shan't be long, driver.

DRIVER: Yes, o.k.

DOORMAN: Can't afford to lose a pair of gloves these days. It isn't (*Start FADE*) just a question of the money, it's a question of the blinkin' coupons.

CUT TO: The Machicha Club Entrance Hall.

TEMPLE returns in a hurry through the swing doors. The orchestra is playing in the background.

WAITER: Is anything the matter, sir?

TEMPLE: (*Crisply*) Where's your telephone?

WAITER: There's a box in the corner, sir, just opposite –

TEMPLE: Thank you!

TEMPLE crosses to the telephone booth, opens the door, squeezes in, closes the door, lifts the receiver, puts coins into the box, and dials.

A pause.

We hear the number ringing out. Then the receiver is lifted at the other end.

FORBES: (*On the other end of the phone*) Hello?

TEMPLE presses button "A".

FORBES: Hello?

95

TEMPLE:	(*On the phone*) Sir Graham?
FORBES:	Oh, hello, Temple!
TEMPLE:	(*Urgently*) Are you alone?
FORBES:	Why, no, I've got Kaufman here …
TEMPLE:	Well, listen – I'm in a desperate hurry and I've got to talk fast. I'm in the Machicha Club. Steve and I are just leaving … Someone's trying to pick us up.
FORBES:	(*Seriously perturbed*) What do you mean – in a taxi?
TEMPLE:	Yes.
FORBES:	Are you sure?
TEMPLE:	Pretty sure. Have you got a car handy?
FORBES:	Kaufman has.
TEMPLE:	Good. Now listen, I'm deliberately going to fall for it, but I want you to follow us.
FORBES:	Where is the Machicha Club – Berkeley Square?
TEMPLE:	Yes.
FORBES:	Good. We'll be there in five or six minutes.
TEMPLE:	Right. The number of the cab is DHO 838.
FORBES:	Stall him for as long as you can!
TEMPLE:	Yes, all right!

TEMPLE replaces the receiver, opens the door of the telephone booth, and moves across the hall. In his hurry, he bumps into someone.

TEMPLE:	Oh, I'm sorry, I –
MRS FORESTER:	Why, good evening, Mr Temple!
TEMPLE:	Oh – hello, Mrs Forester!

MRS FORESTER:(*Faintly amused*) You appear to be in rather a hurry?

TEMPLE: Yes, I – I had to make a telephone call.

MRS FORESTER:(*Curious; watching TEMPLE*) So I gathered. Are you alone?

TEMPLE: No, my wife's outside. She's – waiting for me.

MRS FORESTER:Oh.

TEMPLE: We're just leaving.

MRS FORESTER:Oh, what a pity!

TEMPLE: I had a feeling that I might possibly bump into you this evening.

MRS FORESTER:Did you? What made you think that?

TEMPLE: Oh, I don't know. Perhaps seeing Joseph here.

MRS FORESTER:Seeing Joseph?

TEMPLE: Yes. You appear to be surprised, Mrs Forester.

MRS FORESTER:Where is Joseph?

TEMPLE: Why, here – at the Machicha.

MRS FORESTER:(*Apparently astonished*) Here? Do you mean to say that Joseph is – Are you sure?

TEMPLE: Quite sure. I spoke to him.

MRS FORESTER:Well, really, this is too much. You have to pay your servants the earth these days and then when you pay them the earth … Oh, really, this is exasperating!

TEMPLE: (*Politely: pulling her leg*) Shall I ask him to leave?

MRS FORESTER:(*Taking TEMPLE seriously*)No, you can't very well ask – (*Suddenly, laughing*) Oh, I can see the funny side

97

of it, but really it is so annoying! Ah, well – goodnight – Mr Temple.

TEMPLE: Goodbye, Mrs Forester!

CUT TO: The Street outside the Club.

The taxi engine is ticking over.

DRIVER: He's taking 'is blinkin' time!

DOORMAN: Here he is, madam!

STEVE: Oh, good.

TEMPLE arrives, very leisurely. He is whistling.

STEVE: You've been a very long time, darling.

TEMPLE: Have I?

DOORMAN: Did you find your gloves, sir?

TEMPLE: M'm? Oh, yes. Yes, thanks very much. I dropped them in the cloakroom.

DOORMAN: You were lucky, sir.

TEMPLE: Yes. Yes, rather.

STEVE: Jump in, Pau!

DRIVER: Where to?

TEMPLE: Take us to … Steve, how would you like to go to Pinolios for an hour or so?

STEVE: Not at this time of night, darling.

TEMPLE: Oh, why not, it's early yet!

STEVE: (*Firmly*) No. The flat!

TEMPLE: (*Brightly*) All right, but I think you're making a terrible mistake! (*To the DRIVER*) Half Moon Street.

DRIVER: O.K.!

TEMPLE: You can drop us on the corner you know, near –

DRIVER: Yes, all right!

DOORMAN: Goodnight, sir!

TEMPLE: Oh, em, here we are …

STEVE: (*Quietly*) You have tipped him, Paul.

TEMPLE: Oh, have I? Oh well – (*He gets into the taxi*) Goodnight!

The DOORMAN closes the taxi door.

DOORMAN: Goodnight, sir!

The taxi drives away and gathers speed.

STEVE: Paul, what's the matter with you?

TEMPLE: What do you mean?

STEVE: You're dithering about like an old man!

TEMPLE: Don't be silly! Are you comfy over there?

STEVE: Yes, of course I am! Darling, is anything the matter?

TEMPLE: (*Quietly*) Yes.

STEVE: What?

TEMPLE: This taxi was waiting for us.

STEVE: What do you mean?

TEMPLE: You know what I mean, darling.

STEVE: You mean he deliberately – Oh, nonsense.

TEMPLE: All right – we'll soon see.

STEVE: Paul, you … you don't really think that – (*She stops*)

TEMPLE: Well?

A moment.

STEVE: (*Thoughtfully*) It was rather odd, wasn't it?

TEMPLE: He ought to take the next turning, if he intends to – There you are. There you are – he missed it …

STEVE: Paul, where's he taking us to?

TEMPLE: Your guess is as good as mine.

STEVE: But what are we going to do?

TEMPLE: It's all right, Steve.

STEVE: Paul, supposing he – (*She stops; the taxi is gathering speed*) He's going faster!

TEMPLE: Yes … Steve, what are you taking your shoe off for?

99

STEVE:	We've got to break the window.
TEMPLE:	No! No! Steve, wait. I want to know where he's taking us to.
STEVE:	But, Paul, we can't just sit here and – Darling, that's ridiculous.
TEMPLE:	(*A tense whisper*) Steve, turn round. Look through the window at the back …
STEVE:	Is that car following us?
TEMPLE:	Yes; it's Sir Graham.
STEVE:	What? … Oh, you didn't lose your gloves! You telephoned him; that's why you went back.
TEMPLE:	Yes.
STEVE:	Who's behind all this, darling – Belasco?
TEMPLE:	(*Thoughtfully*) Yes.
STEVE:	I wonder where we're going?
TEMPLE:	He'll begin to think it rather off if we don't start kicking up a fuss. Sit back, darling …
STEVE:	What are you going to do?

PAUL bangs on the glass partition.

TEMPLE:	I say! I say, I told you to go to Half Moon Street! (*The DRIVER doesn't reply*) What the devil is the idea? D'you hear me? (*Shouting*) D'you hear me! I told you to go to Half Moon Street!
STEVE:	(*Softly*) Now we know that you were right.
TEMPLE:	Yes.
STEVE:	He's accelerating.
TEMPLE:	You know, this – (*He stops*)
STEVE:	What is it?
TEMPLE:	I can't see the car behind …
STEVE:	Oh, no. Don't say we've lost them.
TEMPLE:	No. No. No. There they are.

STEVE: Who's with Sir Graham?

TEMPLE: Philip Kaufman … You know, Steve, this business is peculiar. After I left you, and went back to telephone, I bumped bang slap into Mrs Forester –

There is a noise in the background; rather like a car back-firing. The taxi starts to swerve.

STEVE: What was that?

TEMPLE: What?

STEVE: That noise?

TEMPLE: It was a car back-firing.

STEVE: Oh. I've lost my shoe, darling, I had it in my hand a moment ago … What's happening?

TEMPLE: He's swerving all over the place, what the devil is he doing?

The taxi starts to brake.

STEVE: Paul, what … what's the matter? What is it?

TEMPLE: I don't know what's happened. Good … good heavens, what's he trying to do!

STEVE: Paul, he's pulling up!

TEMPLE: We're in the middle of the road, surely – By George, you're right, he is pulling up!

The taxi breaks to a standstill. The engine immediately stalls.

STEVE: He's switched his engine off.

TEMPLE: No, it stalled. (*Softly*) What's happened, Steve?

STEVE: He's leaning over the wheel as if he's fainted or something.

TEMPLE: Wait a minute. (*Struggling with the door handle*) I can't – get this confounded door open – Ah, that's it!

101

The door opens and TEMPLE gets out.

TEMPLE: Come on, Steve …

The sound of a fast-approaching car.

STEVE: I've lost my shoe somewhere …

TEMPLE: Here's Sir Graham!

The car races up and brakes to a standstill. The sound of car doors opening and closing as Sir GRAHAM and KAUFMAN get out.

STEVE: I don't know where my shoe is …

TEMPLE: (*Ignoring Steve*) Hello, Sir Graham!

FORBES: (*Arriving*) What happened?

KAUFMAN: Are you both all right?

TEMPLE: Yes, thanks.

FORBES: I can't imagine what happened! He suddenly stared to swerve all over the place and then pulled up!

KAUFMAN: (*From the front of the taxi*) I say!

FORBES: What is it?

KAUFMAN: The driver seems to be in a pretty bad way!

FORBES: I should imagine he must have had a seizure.

TEMPLE: Give me your hand, Steve! I'll help you out.

STEVE: Paul, I've lost my shoe.

TEMPLE: (*Impatiently, offering his hand*) Come along, darling … That's it.

STEVE reluctantly gets out of the taxi.

KAUFMAN: Mr Temple! Sir Graham! Come over here a moment, please!

TEMPLE and SIR GRAHAM join KAUFMAN.

FORBES: What is it, Kaufman?

KAUFMAN: Take a look at this man. Look at his face …

FORBES:	Why, he's been shot.
TEMPLE:	That accounts for it! That accounts for the cab suddenly swerving. Steve said she thought she heard something. I thought it was a car back-firing, but – Sir Graham, don't you see what happened?
KAUFMAN:	Someone must have known we were following the cab. They waited, most probably in a shop doorway, until the cab got level with them.
FORBES:	But how could they know?
KAUFMAN:	Where did you telephone from?
TEMPLE:	From the Machicha.
KAUFMAN:	From the callbox?
TEMPLE:	Yes, there was a callbox in the hall.

The TAXI DRIVER starts to moan. He is seriously injured and in pain.

FORBES:	I say, we'll have to get an ambulance for this fellow.
KAUFMAN:	Wait a moment! I believe he's trying to say something.
STEVE:	(*Drawing nearer*) Is he badly hurt?
TEMPLE:	Darling, don't come too near, I don't want you to see him …
FORBES:	It'll only upset you, Steve.
STEVE:	But can't I do anything?
TEMPLE:	No, no, Steve – please!

The DRIVER continues to moan.

KAUFMAN:	Temple, he's trying to say something!

The DRIVER tries to speak, but he is in pain and his words are inaudible.

FORBES:	What is it?
TEMPLE:	I don't know.
KAUFMAN:	What is he trying to say?

TEMPLE: I don't know, unless – (*He kneels down beside the DRIVER*) Now look here, old man – just relax. That's it, that's it … That's better. (*Gently*) Now, where were you going to take us to?

DRIVER: I was told to take you to … to …

TEMPLE: Yes?

DRIVER: … to take … you … to …

TEMPLE: Yes?

DRIVER: … to …

With almost a final gasp of breath he announces a name which is so inaudible it might be ABELSTONE – or even ABELSDON.

FORBES: He's dead.

TEMPLE: Yes.

STEVE gives a quick, horrified, start of surprise.

FORBES: What did he say?

KAUFMAN: What was it? "I was told to take you to Abelstone."

FORBES: Abelstone?

TEMPLE: It sounded more like Abelsdon to me.

FORBES: That's what I thought!

KAUFMAN: Abelsdon? Is there a place called Abelsdon?

TEMPLE: Not that I know of.

The sound of an approaching police car is heard.

FORBES: (*Puzzled*) I wonder if that's what he said?

KAUFMAN: He spoke so indistinctly, I don't know …

TEMPLE: Here are two of your men by the look of things.

FORBES: Yes, it's a patrol car.

The patrol car draws up to the kerb. The doors open and two policemen get out.

TEMPLE: (*Not really thinking of what he is saying*) Are you all right, Steve?

STEVE: Yes, but Paul, I've only got one shoe, and I … I can't very well –

STEVE is interrupted by the arrival of SERGEANT O'DAY.

O'DAY: What the devil's goin' on here?

FORBES: Oh, good evening, Sergeant. There's been an accident and –

O'DAY: An accident, did you say? Is there anyone hurt now?

FORBES: Yes – the driver's been killed.

BRADDOCK: Ah … Well, if you take the particulars, Sergeant, I'll – Oh! (*Springing to attention and saluting*) I'm sorry, sir. I … I didn't recognise you.

O'DAY: Recognise? What the devil are you blathering on – Oh, I … I beg your pardon, Sir Graham.

FORBES: That's all right, Sergeant.

O'DAY: Sergeant O'Day, sir.

BRADDOCK: P.C. Braddock, sir.

TEMPLE: Sergeant, do you know this district very well?

O'DAY: Why, yes, sir.

TEMPLE: Do you happen to know a place called Abelsdon?

O'DAY: What sort of a place, sir?

TEMPLE: I don't know. It might be a shop, it might be a club, it might be a private house even.

O'DAY: Abelsdon?

TEMPLE: Yes.

O'DAY: I'm afraid I don't, sir. What about you, George?

BRADDOCK: Sorry, sir.

TEMPLE: Well – do you know a person called Abelsdon?

O'DAY: A person?

TEMPLE: Yes.

O'DAY: I'm afraid I don't, sir.

BRADDOCK: Sorry, sir.

KAUFMAN: What about the name Abelstone?

BRADDOCK: Abelstone, sir?

KAUFMAN: Yes.

FORBES: Does that mean anything to you?

BRADDOCK: (*A moment*) I … I'm afraid it doesn't, sir.

FORBES: Sergeant?

O'DAY: No, sir.

FORBES: M'm. Well, it rather looks to me as if we're on the wrong track.

BRADDOCK: Begging your pardon, sir, but – how do you spell that name?

FORBES: Spell it?

BRADDOCK: Yes, sir.

FORBES: Well …

TEMPLE: What makes you ask that?

BRADDOCK: Well, I was just thinking, sir. Are you quite sure the name is Abelsdon or Abelstone?

TEMPLE: No, we're not sure – that's just the point.

FORBES: This man – the taxi driver – was taking Mr and Mrs Temple to an unknown destination. Just before he died, he said what sounded to us remarkably like "I was told to take you to Abelsdon".

BRADDOCK: I take it the point is, sir, that you've got to find that place – or person?

FORBES: Exactly.

106

TEMPLE: What's on your mind, officer?

BRADDOCK: Well, the name the taxi driver said, sir – Could it have been Dunne, sir – Abel Dunne?

TEMPLE: Abel Dunne?

BRADDOCK: Yes, sir.

KAUFMAN: No. No, I don't think so.

TEMPLE: Abel Dunne – I'm not so sure.

FORBES: No. No, neither am I.

TEMPLE: Who is Abel Dunne?

O'DAY: He's a Welshman, sir. Only a youngish chap – he runs a small dry-cleaning business in Layman Street.

TEMPLE: Layman Street?

BRADDOCK: It's about half a mile from here, sir.

TEMPLE: In which direction?

BRADDOCK: You were going in the right direction, sir.

O'DAY: We've had our eye on his place for some time, sir. There's something queer going on there but we just don't know what it is.

FORBES: What do you mean exactly – something queer?

O'DAY: Well, Dunne seems to receive an awful lot of visitors and they don't always belong to the district, as you might say, sir. Secondly, he seems to make a great deal of money but – well – he's not exactly interested in the business.

BRADDOCK: (*Significantly*) Not in the dry-cleaning business.

FORBES: M'm. Have you reported this matter?

O'DAY: No, sir, but we're keeping our eyes open.

FORBES: (*Decisively*) Take us to this place, Braddock.

BRADDOCK:	Yes, sir.
FORBES:	Stay here, Sergeant, and take charge.
O'DAY:	Very good, sir.
FORBES:	Ready, Temple?
TEMPLE:	Yes.
STEVE:	Darling, I've lost my shoe!
TEMPLE:	Come along, Steve!
FORBES:	Kaufman, you go along with Braddock – I'll take Mr and Mrs Temple in your car.
KAUFMAN:	Very good, sir.
FORBES:	Come along, Steve.
STEVE:	I've lost my shoe, Sir Graham.
TEMPLE:	Don't hop about, Steve.
STEVE:	(*Raising her voice*) I've lost my shoe!
FORBES:	What?!
TEMPLE:	(*Suddenly aware of STEVE*) You've lost what, darling?
STEVE:	I've – lost – my – shoe!
TEMPLE:	You've lost your shoe?
STEVE:	Yes, darling!
KAUFMAN:	(*Bewildered*) Your shoe?
STEVE:	(*Exasperated*) Yes, my shoe!
KAUFMAN:	Shoe! Mon Dieu! But you can't have lost your shoe –
TEMPLE:	It's ridiculous, Steve, you can't possibly –
STEVE:	I tell you I've lost my shoe!
O'DAY:	Beggin' your pardon, Ma'am.
FORBES:	What is it, Sergeant?
O'DAY:	Is this the article you've been troubling your head about?
STEVE:	Why, yes, that's my – (*Lapsing into broad Irish*) Sergeant, you're a man after my own heart! Will you be putting it on me foot now?

O'DAY: I will that!
TEMPLE laughs.
Play Incidental Music.

CUT TO: LAYMAN STREET.
The patrol car draws up, followed by KAUFMAN's car.
The engines are turned off and door opens.
BRADDOCK: That's the place, sir – on the corner.
TEMPLE: Does Dunne live there?
BRADDOCK: I believe so, sir – there's a small flat above
                  the shop. The entrance to the flat is on the
                  right, sir.
FORBES: M'm. Kaufman?
KAUFMAN: Yes, Sir Graham?
FORBES: Stay here with Mrs Temple and Braddock
                  – if we're not back in five minutes you
                  know what to do.
KAUFMAN: Yes, sir.
FORBES: Come along, Temple …

CUT TO: The Pavement outside the Dry Cleaners.
TEMPLE is pressing a bell-push. In the distant
background a bell rings.
FORBES: He's not in.
TEMPLE: M'm.
TEMPLE stops ringing.
FORBES: Is the door locked?
TEMPLE: (*Trying the door*) Yes, I'm afraid so.
FORBES: Well, that's that.
TEMPLE takes out a bunch of keys.
TEMPLE: Wait a minute …
TEMPLE tries several keys: suddenly he forces the door
open, but the key snaps.
TEMPLE: … No … No … Ah …

FORBES: Have you done it?

TEMPLE: Yes, but I've broken the damn key! It – that's a nuisance!

TEMPLE pushes open the door.

FORBES: There's a narrow staircase – the flat must be at the top.

TEMPLE: Yes.

FORBES: (*Closing the door*) Let me go first, Temple.

TEMPLE: All right.

FORBES and TEMPLE start to climb the stairs.

TEMPLE: Can you see?

FORBES: Not too well, I'm afraid.

Suddenly FORBES slips.

FORBES: Damn!

TEMPLE: Did you hurt yourself?

FORBES: No.

TEMPLE: What made you slip?

FORBES: I don't know, I think I put my foot on something, I … Wait a minute! (*Grasping on the stairs*) Yes … Yes, yes, here we are …

TEMPLE: What is it?

FORBES: I don't know, it feels like a piece of metal or something.

TEMPLE: Wait a minute, I'll strike a match.

TEMPLE feels in his pocket for matches.

FORBES: Temple, I believe it's – (*TEMPLE strikes a match*) Why, yes! Look, it's a cigarette lighter – it's a lighter exactly like the one you found on Ross Morgan!

TEMPLE: Let me have a look at it!

FORBES: What are you looking at?

TEMPLE: This is the lighter Steve had. The one I returned to David Nelson.

FORBES: The identical one?

TEMPLE: Yes.

FORBES: Are you sure?

TEMPLE: Quite sure.

FORBES: How do you know?

TEMPLE: Well, look – there's a tiny scratch on the corner, near the flint.

FORBES: Well?

TEMPLE: I had a hunch that sooner or later this lighter would turn up again, that's why I made quite sure that when it did, I'd recognise it.

FORBES: What do you mean?

TEMPLE: I made this mark myself, Sir Graham.

FORBES: Then Nelson must have been here!

TEMPLE: It looks very much like it, unless – (*He stops: quietly*) What was that?

FORBES: What?

TEMPLE: I thought I heard something.

FORBES: No, I don't think so.

TEMPLE: Come along, Sir Graham. Let's go upstairs.

TEMPLE and FORBES continue upstairs and reach the door of the flat.

FORBES: (*Softly*) Here we are …

A moment.

TEMPLE: I don't hear anything. You know, I don't think there's anyone in.

FORBES: No, I don't think there is. The door's locked.

TEMPLE: Are you sure?

FORBES: (*Trying to open the door*) Yes … Ah …

TEMPLE: What is it?

FORBES: There's something on the doorknob, I think it's – (*He stops*)

TEMPLE: It's blood … Get the door open. Get it open – quickly! Quickly, Sir Graham!

111

TEMPLE and FORBES throw their weight against the door, and it breaks down. They enter the flat.

FORBES: There's another room over there …

FORBES crosses and opens the door.

FORBES: (*Calling*) Temple! Temple!

TEMPLE joins FORBES.

FORBES: Look at this man … Just look at him.

TEMPLE: Oh …

FORBES: He's been beaten up. He's been absolutely beaten up.

TEMPLE: Yes.

FORBES: Who is he – do you know?

TEMPLE: His name's Lord Craymore – he spoke to me about an hour ago at the Machicha.

Closing Music.

END OF EPISODE FOUR

EPISODE FIVE

DAVID NELSON EXPLAINS

OPEN TO:

ANNOUNCER: Paul Temple, the celebrated novelist and private detective, is visited by Sir Graham Forbes of Scotland Yard and by Mr Philip Kaufman who is attached to the Special Branch. Kaufman tells Paul Temple about a notorious criminal known as Dr Belasco. Temple promises to try and discover the identity of Belasco and during the course of certain investigations makes the acquaintance of Henry Worth, David Nelson, Mrs Forester, Joseph – a servant of Mrs Forester's – and a certain Mr Ed Bellamy. Bellamy is the proprietor of the Machicha Club in Berkeley Square. One night, after a visit to the Machicha, Temple and Steve are abducted, and an attempt is made to take them to an address in Layman Street. The attempt fails, however, and later the same night Temple and Sir Graham Forbes visit the address: this turns out to be a small dry cleaner's establishment owned by a man called Abel Dunne. Temple and Forbes force an entrance and make their way (*Start FADE*) up the narrow staircase to the flat which is situated above the shop.

CUT TO: On the Landing by the Flat Door.

TEMPLE: I don't think there's anyone in.

FORBES: No, I don't think there is. The door's locked.

115

TEMPLE: Are you sure?

FORBES: (*Trying to open the door*) Yes … Ah …

TEMPLE: What is it?

FORBES: There's something on the doorknob, I think it's
– (*He stops*)

TEMPLE: It's blood … Get the door open. Get it open –
quickly! Quickly, Sir Graham!

TEMPLE and FORBES throw their weight against the door, and it breaks down. They enter the flat.

FORBES: There's another room over there …

FORBES crosses and opens the door.

FORBES: (*Calling*) Temple! Temple!

TEMPLE joins FORBES.

FORBES: Look at this man … Just look at him.

TEMPLE: Oh …

FORBES: He's been beaten up. He's been absolutely
beaten up.

TEMPLE: Yes.

FORBES: Who is he – do you know?

TEMPLE: His name's Lord Craymore – he spoke to me
about an hour ago at the Machicha.

FORBES: But why should this happen? Why?

TEMPLE: Craymore wanted to see me, and I arranged to
meet him at the flat. He said he wanted to talk
about Dr Belasco.

FORBES: Did he know the identity of Belasco?

TEMPLE: I don't know.

FORBES: M'm. Well, there's nothing we can do for the
poor devil, I'm afraid. He's had it.

TEMPLE: I'm afraid so.

FORBES: Let's go back into the other room, Temple.

FORBES closes the door as they pass into the other room.

TEMPLE: Our friend Mr Dunne doesn't appear to be a
very tidy individual.

116

FORBES: It rather looks to me as if he left in a hurry.

TEMPLE: Yes. Just what I was thinking.

FORBES: You know, Kaufman's right about this business. Someone must have found out about your telephone call. They knew that we were following you and that unless something happened to prevent the driver from bringing –

FORBES is interrupted by the ringing of the telephone.

A tense pause.

The telephone continues to ring for some little time.

FORBES: Well, whoever it is, they're pretty persistent!

TEMPLE: Yes.

The telephone continues to ring.

TEMPLE: I'll take a chance on it.

TEMPLE lifts the receiver.

JOSEPH: (*On the other end of the line*) Grosvenor 6891?

TEMPLE: (*On the phone*) Yes …

JOSEPH: Could I speak to Mr Dunne, please?

TEMPLE: Who is that speaking?

JOSEPH: I'm speaking on behalf of a Mrs Forester.

TEMPLE: Yes?

JOSEPH: I'm given to understand that you – (*He stops; suspicious*) That is Mr Dunne, speaking personally?

TEMPLE: Yes.

JOSEPH: Mr Abel Dunne?

TEMPLE: (*A momentary hesitation*) Yes, speaking.

JOSEPH: Well, I'm given to understand that – (*He stops*)

TEMPLE: Yes?

JOSEPH suddenly replaces the receiver.

FORBES: What's happened?

TEMPLE: It … He's replaced the receiver.

FORBES: Who was it, do you know?

117

TEMPLE: Yes, it's the man I told you about. Joseph. Works for Mrs Forester.

FORBES: But I thought you said you saw him, at the Machicha Club?

TEMPLE: I did – as a matter of fact I spoke to him.

FORBES: Are you sure it was the same man on the phone?

TEMPLE: Yes.

FORBES: But what did he say?

TEMPLE: Well, first of all he said that he was speaking for Mrs Forester, then he asked me if I was Abel Dunne. When I said that I was, he said: "I'm given to understand that you –"; then he stopped – obviously he must have guessed that something was the matter.

FORBES: I wonder what he wanted.

TEMPLE: I don't know.

In the distant background the sound of footsteps can be heard.

FORBES: You know, Temple, Braddock must have been right. This is the place that taxi driver intended to bring you to, otherwise –

TEMPLE: Listen … There's someone coming up the stairs!

FORBES: Yes! (*A moment*) I wonder if it's Kaufman!

TEMPLE: No … No, I don't think it is.

FORBES: (*Quietly*) Stand by the door, Temple.

TEMPLE: Yes, all right.

The footsteps draw nearer.

A pause.

FORBES: (*A low whisper*) He's at the door.

TEMPLE: Yes … don't touch it!

Suddenly the door is thrown open.

WORTH: (*Extremely angry and overwrought*) Stand back! This time, my friend, I've come under slightly different circumstances – (*He stops: bewildered*)

FORBES: (*Politely*) Good evening, Mr Worth.

WORTH: Sir Graham! What does this mean? What's happened? Where's Dunne? (*Astonished: notices Temple*) Mr Temple?

TEMPLE: Drop the gun. Drop it!

WORTH drops the gun.

WORTH: (*Frightened*) What are you doing here?

TEMPLE: What's more to the point – what are you doing here?

WORTH: I came to see Mr Dunne.

TEMPLE: Had you an appointment?

WORTH: No, but … I'm not talking – I'm not saying a word, not until I've seen my solicitor.

TEMPLE: Was Abel Dunne a friend of yours?

WORTH: You heard what I said, I'm not talking!

TEMPLE: Was Abel Dunne a friend of yours? (*Almost bullying WORTH*) Was he?

WORTH: (*Weakly*) No.

TEMPLE: Why did you come here? (*A moment: raising his voice, almost a threat*) Why did you come here?

WORTH: I – I was told to come here by Dr Belasco.

FORBES: When?

WORTH: About – ten days ago.

FORBES: Go on.

A pause.

WORTH refuses to continue.

TEMPLE: Mr Worth, the last time I saw you I asked you about a woman called Mrs Forester. You told me that you'd never been to her house and that you'd never even heard of her. And yet in spite of this –

WORTH: (*Suddenly: desperately*) Mr Temple, you've got to believe me! Please, you've got to believe me! I came here tonight because – Just over a week ago I received a telephone call. I was told that unless I delivered two hundred pounds to this address my café would be smashed to pieces and my business taken away from me.

TEMPLE: You delivered the money?

WORTH: Yes, I was frightened. I … I came here one afternoon.

FORBES: To the flat?

WORTH: No, to the shop down below. I saw a man called Abel Dunne. He was expecting me, and I handed over the two hundred pounds.

TEMPLE: Was Dunne the man you spoke to on the telephone?

WORTH: No, I don't think so.

TEMPLE: Go on.

WORTH: After I'd handed over the money, I realised what a coward, and what a complete fool I'd been. I made up my mind that the next time I heard from Belasco, I'd threaten to expose him unless he returned the two hundred pounds.

TEMPLE: How could you expose him?

WORTH: What do you mean?

TEMPLE: (*Forcefully*) Who is Dr Belasco?

WORTH: (*A little surprised*) Why, obviously this man Dunne – the … the man who took the two hundred pounds!

TEMPLE: You think so?

WORTH: But he must be!

FORBES: Is that why you came here tonight?

120

WORTH: Belasco – or one of his men – telephoned me last night. I was told to bring a hundred pounds.

FORBES: To this address?

WORTH: Yes.

FORBES: Tonight?

WORTH: No, I was supposed to have brought the money first thing this morning. (*Faintly aggressive*) Well, I didn't!

FORBES: (*Completing WORTH's story for him*) Instead, you came here tonight – complete with this little weapon – in order to try and get back your two hundred.

WORTH: (*A little shame-faced*) Yes.

FORBES: You expect us to believe that story?

WORTH: I don't care whether you believe it or not! It's the truth!

FORBES: M'm! Well, it seems to me, Mr Worth, that –

WORTH: (*Interrupting FORBES*) What's that?

From below we hear the voice of PHILIP KAUFMAN.

KAUFMAN: (*Calling*) Sir Graham! Mr Temple! Are you all right?

TEMPLE: It's Kaufman … and Braddock.

TEMPLE opens the door. KAUFMAN and PC BRADDOCK arrive.

KAUFMAN: We saw Worth arrive, sir – so we thought we'd better see if you were all right?

FORBES: We're all right; but I'm afraid our mysterious friend Mr Dunne hasn't put in an appearance.

KAUFMAN: No, and I don't think he will either, Sir Graham – not tonight.

TEMPLE: Why do you say that?

KAUFMAN: (*To BRADDOCK*) Tell them!

BRADDOCK: There's been an emergency call from the Yard, sir.

FORBES: Well?

BRADDOCK: A lorry was stolen from Fenchurch Street about three quarters of an hour ago; the description of the driver fits Abel Dunne to a T.

FORBES: What was on the lorry?

KAUFMAN: Cigarettes.

TEMPLE: Cigarettes?

KAUFMAN: Three and a half million of them, Mr Temple - £17,000 worth.

TEMPLE: By Timothy!

WORTH: Seventeen thousand! Didn't I tell you! Didn't I tell you that Dunne was Dr Belasco!

KAUFMAN is amused: he starts laughing.

WORTH: Why are you laughing?

KAUFMAN: Stupidity always makes me laugh, my friend! Especially when it is assumed stupidity!

WORTH: What do you mean?

KAUFMAN: You know perfectly well what I mean! Belasco's behind this business, we know that – but he didn't drive the lorry, my friend.

WORTH: How do you know?

KAUFMAN: Because I'm pretty sure that Mr Dunne drove the lorry and Mr Dunne is not, I assure you, Dr Belasco. Incidentally, Mr Worth – what exactly are you doing here tonight?

WORTH: I've already explained my presence here to Sir Graham.

KAUFMAN: Have you? I feel sure that what your explanation lacked in conviction it made up in originality.

TEMPLE: Why do you think Mr Worth came here tonight?

KAUFMAN: Isn't it obvious?

FORBES: What do you mean, Kaufman?

KAUFMAN: Worth knew about the lorry. Even if he isn't Belasco, it's quite obvious that he helped to plan the whole business.

WORTH, furious, completely loses control of himself and strides out.

WORTH: That's a lie! That's a filthy, dirty lie!

BRADDOCK: (*Holding WORTH*) Now, sir! Now, sir! None of that, sir!

WORTH: (*A moment; regaining his breath*) I've only seen this man once in my life – that was the time I told you about – the time I handed over the two hundred pounds.

TEMPLE: Did you see Dunne alone – on that occasion?

WORTH: (*Hesitating*) Yes.

TEMPLE: Quite alone?

WORTH: Yes, he was alone, but …

FORBES: But what?

WORTH: I was just thinking …

FORBES: Well?

WORTH: After I'd handed over the two hundred pounds, he told me to go. I went outside into the corridor, but, instead of going straight into the road, I stood by the door – listening.

FORBES: Well?

WORTH: He made a telephone call – a personal call to a man called Allen.

FORBES: You don't remember the number?

WORTH: Yes. It was a trunk call – Greenchurch 87.

BRADDOCK: Greenchurch 87?

WORTH: Yes.

FORBES: What is it, Braddock?

BRADDOCK: Well, that … that's the Cromwell Heart, sir.

FORBES: The Cromwell Heart?

BRADDOCK: It's a pub – an inn, sir – at Greenchurch.

FORBES: Do you know the place?

BRADDOCK: I ought to, sir. I was born pretty well next door to it.

FORBES: Where is Greenchurch?

TEMPLE: It's about eighteen miles from Willesborough – on the Romney marshes.

BRADDOCK: That's right, sir.

KAUFMAN: This telephone conversation, Mr Worth, that you so conveniently overheard.

WORTH: Yes?

KAUFMAN: (*Snapping at WORTH*) Well – what was the gist of it?

WORTH: Dunne simply informed this man Allen that I had delivered the two hundred pounds.

KAUFMAN: That's all he said?

WORTH: That's all I heard him say, Mr Kaufman!

KAUFMAN: M'm.

FORBES: What sort of place is this Greenchurch?

BRADDOCK: It's just a fair-size village, sir.

TEMPLE: I wonder if Belasco's got a hide-out down there and that's where they've taken the lorry.

FORBES: That's just what I was thinking! I've a good mind to contact the Yard and send Perry down. (*A moment*) Braddock …

BRADDOCK: Yes, sir?

FORBES: Are you well-known in that part of the world?

BRADDOCK: Greenchurch, sir?

FORBES: Yes.

BRADDOCK: Oh, no, sir. You see, I've been away for years.

FORBES: But you know the district?

BRADDOCK: Like the palm of my hand, sir.

FORBES: Who's in charge of your Division?

BRADDOCK: Inspector Copthorne, sir.

FORBES: Good! I'll get Perry to speak to Copthorne first thing tomorrow; meanwhile change into plain clothes and get down to Greenchurch. Keep your wits about you and your eyes open. If you see anything out of the ordinary, report direct to the Yard.

BRADDOCK: Very good, sir.

FORBES: Report to Mr Kaufman or Inspector Perry – you understand?

BRADDOCK: Yes, sir! I understand, sir.

Play Incidental Music.

CUT TO: The Hallway of the TEMPLES' Flat.

The door buzzer is sounded. CHARLIE approaches and opens the door.

CHARLIE: Good evening, sir!

TEMPLE: Hello, Charlie!

TEMPLE and STEVE enter, and CHARLIE shuts the door.

CHARLIE: I'll take the coat, Ma'am.

STEVE: Ah, thank you.

TEMPLE: Any messages?

CHARLIE: Mr Nelson's here, sir – he's in the lounge, sir.

TEMPLE: Mr Nelson?

STEVE: How long has he been here?

CHARLIE: Oh, only about two or three minutes. Seems in a bit of a stew with himself. Would you like me to get you any sandwiches or something?

TEMPLE moves to the lounge door.

TEMPLE: No thank you, Charlie.

Cross to the lounge. The door opens, TEMPLE enters, followed by STEVE.

TEMPLE: Hello, Nelson!

NELSON: Oh, good evening, sir! (*Pleasantly*) Hello, Mrs Temple. How are you?

STEVE: I'm very well. Thank you.

NELSON: I'm sorry bursting in on you like this – please forgive me.

STEVE: Is anything the matter, Mr Nelson?

NELSON: Yes – I'm afraid I've had rather an unfortunate experience.

TEMPLE: Don't tell me you've had another motor car accident!

NELSON: No, it's nothing like that Temple, but – well – as a matter of fact, I've had my flat burgled.

TEMPLE: Your flat burgled?

NELSON: Yes.

TEMPLE: When?

126

NELSON: (*Watching TEMPLE*) Some time this afternoon – it must have happened between half-past three and five o'clock.

TEMPLE: You told the police?

NELSON: Yes, of course, naturally ... Oh, I see what you mean! You're wondering why I've taken the trouble to come along here? Well – as a matter of fact, Temple – the whole business is rather odd. You see, the place was quite obviously ransacked and yet very little was stolen. It almost looks to me as if they were searching for something.

TEMPLE: What did they take?

NELSON: A wallet – rather a nice wallet as a matter of fact – a pair of gold cuff links and a small bedroom clock.

TEMPLE: That's all.

NELSON: Yes, yes that's all. Oh – and a cigarette lighter.

TEMPLE: Your cigarette lighter?

NELSON: Yes – it's the one my wife had. You remember, the one that Mrs Temple borrowed.

TEMPLE: Yes, I remember. Why do you think this business is rather odd, Mr Nelson?

NELSON: Well, don't you think it is?

TEMPLE: There's quite a lot of this sort of thing going on just now, it's not exactly unique.

NELSON: Yes, but surely ...

TEMPLE: (*Politely*) Yes?

NELSON: Well, I was going to say, surely you believe there's a connection; between what

127

happened this afternoon and the Belasco affair?

TEMPLE: Why should I believe it?

NELSON is faintly bewildered by TEMPLE's attitude.

NELSON: Surely … Temple, don't you realise that since Mary Hamilton was murdered, since I decided to take a personal interest in this affair, there have been two attempts on my life, two definite attempts –

TEMPLE: (*Interrupting NELSON*) Nelson …

NELSON: (*Surprised*) Yes?

TEMPLE: Supposing we put our cards on the table?

NELSON: What do you mean?

TEMPLE: Supposing you tell me exactly what you think happened this afternoon.

A pause.

NELSON: All right. (*Frankly*) I think my flat was broken into by Mrs Forester – or someone acting on Mrs Forester's behalf. I believe that that person was told to get the letters that Mrs Forester wrote to my wife. I believe, quite frankly, that Mrs Forester is the person you're looking for – the notorious Dr Belasco!

TEMPLE: Well, that's frank enough – now I'll be frank with you. Here's your cigarette lighter.

NELSON: How on earth – Do you mean to say – Is this a joke?

TEMPLE: Isn't it your lighter?

NELSON: Of course, it's my lighter, you know perfectly well it is … You searched my flat. You broke into my flat this afternoon and –

STEVE starts to laugh.

STEVE: Do you really think that's what happened, Mr Nelson?

NELSON: Well, if it isn't, where did you get the lighter from?

TEMPLE: I found it – or rather, Sir Graham Forbes found it.

NELSON: Where?

TEMPLE: (*Watching NELSON*) At Mr Dunne's.

NELSON: Who the devil's Mr Dunne?

TEMPLE: He's the proprietor of a small dry-cleaning establishment in Layman Street.

NELSON: You must forgive me if I appear a little bewildered, Temple, but – quite frankly – I can't make head nor tail of this!

TEMPLE: We found your lighter on a staircase – leading up to a flat occupied by a certain Mr Abel Dunne. We assumed, not unnaturally, that you had visited Mr Dunne and accidentally dropped your lighter.

NELSON: But I've never even heard of the man – (*He stops: suddenly, softly*) Just a minute. Look here, you can see what's happened. This is the man Mrs Forester engaged – the man who broke into the flat. When he found that he couldn't find the letters he grew desperate and decided to help himself to –

STEVE: The cigarette lighter, the wallet and the clock.

NELSON: Exactly, Mrs Temple! You didn't see the wallet, I suppose, or the clock?

TEMPLE: No – and if we had we shouldn't have known they were yours.

NELSON: No, no, of course not! (*Suddenly; anxious*) Temple, why did you visit this man Dunne in the first place?

TEMPLE: Because we had reason to believe –

NELSON: He's mixed up in the Belasco affair?

TEMPLE: Yes.

NELSON: (*Pleased with himself*) Well, there's your answer! He's the man who broke into my flat all right. Catch Mr Dunne – (*A sudden thought*) I presume you haven't caught him?

TEMPLE: Not yet.

NELSON: Well, catch Mr Dunne and to my way of thinking you've got the key to the whole situation. Ten to one he'll double-cross Mrs Forester and confess.

TEMPLE: To your way of thinking – we've got Dr Belasco.

NELSON: Exactly.

TEMPLE: M'm. Well – How would you like a drink, Mr Nelson?

NELSON: (*Going*) No thanks, I must be off. As a matter of fact, I feel I'm making rather a nuisance of myself   –

The telephone commences to ring.

TEMPLE: Nonsense!

STEVE: It's all right, Paul – I'll answer it.

NELSON: Goodbye, Mrs Temple!

STEVE: Oh – goodbye, Mr Nelson!

In the background the front door opens and closes as NELSON leaves.

STEVE: (*Lifting the receiver; on the phone*) Hello?

OPERATOR: (*On the other end of the phone*) Mayfair 1784?

STEVE: Yes?

OPERATOR: Hold the line, please – Mr Bellamy wants you!

BELLAMY: (*Coming on the line*) Hello, there!

STEVE: Hello? Mr Bellamy?

BELLAMY: (*Bright and breezy*) Mrs Temple?

STEVE: Yes.

BELLAMY: How are you?

STEVE: I'm very well, Mr Bellamy, thank you. How are you?

BELLAMY: I'm swell. Sorry I didn't get a chance to have a chat with you tonight, Mrs Temple, but – well – you know how it is!

STEVE: I know! Do you want Paul?

BELLAMY: Yes; I'd rather like to have a word with him, if it's convenient.

STEVE: Hold on a moment – (*Aside to TEMPLE*) It's Mr Bellamy.

TEMPLE: Bellamy? (*He takes the receiver*) Hello – Bellamy?

BELLAMY: (*Not quite so bright now*) Hello, Temple, I'm sorry to disturb you.

TEMPLE: That's all right. What can I do for you?

BELLAMY: Well – a rather curious thing happened, after you left the club, Mr Temple. I thought perhaps you might like to hear about it.

TEMPLE: Yes?

BELLAMY: You remember that man we talked about – the man who asked me about Dr Belasco?

TEMPLE: M'm – M'm – I remember.

131

BELLAMY:	Well, shortly after you left, he was joined by a friend of his – a woman. I enquired who she was, and I was told that – (*He laughs*)
TEMPLE:	Yes?
BELLAMY:	I was told that she was Mrs Forester.
TEMPLE:	Well?
BELLAMY:	(*Incredulous*) Well, didn't you tell me that he worked for a Mrs Forester.
TEMPLE:	Yes.
BELLAMY:	(*Laughing*) Nice work if you can get it!
TEMPLE:	What do you mean?
BELLAMY:	They seem to get on like a house on fire – laughing and talking. You sure you haven't got hold of the wrong end of the stick?
TEMPLE:	The wrong end of the stick?
BELLAMY:	Yeah – I mean – are you sure they're not engaged or something?
TEMPLE:	(*Ignoring BELLAMY's question*) Bellamy, tell me: did Mrs Forester go straight across to his table?
BELLAMY:	She sure did. And boy was he glad to see her!
TEMPLE:	M'm. (*A moment*) What time did they leave?
BELLAMY:	They're still here.
TEMPLE:	Are you sure?
BELLAMY:	Sure I'm sure! As a matter of fact, I can see them right now – they're dancing together.
TEMPLE:	(*Surprised*) Dancing together?
BELLAMY:	Yeah – that's what I mean!
TEMPLE:	O.K., Bellamy – thanks for ringing.

BELLAMY: You're welcome. Oh, Mr Temple!

TEMPLE: Yes?

BELLAMY: This guy Joseph.

TEMPLE: Well?

BELLAMY: He wouldn't be Dr Belasco, by any chance?

TEMPLE: (*Laughing*) Your guess is as good as mine, Mr Bellamy.

BELLAMY: (*His tone implies "so you won't talk"*) O.K.! Goodbye.

TEMPLE: Goodbye.

TEMPLE replaces the receiver.

STEVE: What did he want?

TEMPLE: (*His thought elsewhere*) M'm?

STEVE: I said: What did he want, darling?

TEMPLE: Yes, that's just the point – what <u>did</u> he want?

Play Incidental Music.

CUT TO: The TEMPLES' Bathroom.

TEMPLE is having a bath. He's adding more hot water and attempting to sing "Open the Door Richard!" Steve knocks on the door.

STEVE: Paul!

TEMPLE stops singing.

TEMPLE: What is it?

STEVE: Sir Graham's here!

TEMPLE: I can't hear you!

STEVE opens the door.

STEVE: Paul, turn the tap off. Sir Graham's here!

TEMPLE: Oh –

TEMPLE turns the tap off.

TEMPLE: What does he want – do you know?

STEVE: I think he wants to have a word with you about that man Braddock – the young fellow that went down to Greenchurch.

TEMPLE: Oh. Well … you'd better send him in here.

STEVE: (*Laughing as she goes*) Yes, all right!

TEMPLE splashes about. Then SIR GRAHAM appears at the door.

FORBES: Can I come in?

TEMPLE: Oh, yes! Come in, Sir Graham.

FORBES: I could have waited until you'd had your bath, Temple.

TEMPLE: No need for you to wait. Sit down.

FORBES: Thanks. Temple, you know that young fellow I sent down to Greenchurch – the day before yesterday?

TEMPLE: Yes?

FORBES: Well – I got a rather peculiar telegram from him this morning; quite frankly, I don't know what to make of it.

TEMPLE: What's it say?

SIR GRAHAM takes out the telegram and offers it to TEMPLE.

FORBES: Well, here it is.

TEMPLE: No, you read it, Sir Graham.

FORBES: It was handed in at Greenchurch just after eight o'clock this morning. It says: "Important development. Suggest you or Mrs Temple meet me here Britannia Café 3.45. Braddock".

TEMPLE: That's all?

FORBES: Yes.

TEMPLE: Where did he send it to – the Yard?

FORBES: No, as a matter of fact, he sent it to my private address.

TEMPLE: M'm. Where's Constable Braddock staying – the Cromwell Heart?

FORBES: Yes, he's staying there under the name of Bennett.

TEMPLE: Have you mentioned this telegram to Kaufman or Inspector Perry?

FORBES: Not yet. I can't imagine why he didn't send it to Kaufman in the first place.

TEMPLE: M'm. Pass the towel.

FORBES: Well – what do you suggest we do?

TEMPLE: There's only one thing we can do, Sir Graham.

FORBES: Go down to Greenchurch?

TEMPLE: Go down to Greenchurch.

Play Incidental Music.

CUT TO: Upstairs at the Britannia Café, Greenchurch.

There are café noises and chatter, and a small café orchestra. The orchestra stops to a smattering of applause.

TEMPLE: Another cake, darling?

STEVE: No, thank you. Sir Graham?

FORBES: (*His thoughts elsewhere*) No, thank you, Steve. What time do you make it?

TEMPLE: It's nearly five.

FORBES: He's not going to show up.

TEMPLE: I'm afraid not.

FORBES: I wonder – (*He stops*)

TEMPLE: Yes?

FORBES: Oh, I was just thinking: I wonder what we'd better do?

TEMPLE: I don't know.

STEVE: You don't think Braddock left a message for us?

TEMPLE: Here?

STEVE: Well, actually I was thinking of the inn.

135

TEMPLE:	No, he didn't leave a message at the inn, I asked when we arrived.
STEVE:	Well, do you think he left a message here?
FORBES:	I doubt whether he'd do that.
TEMPLE:	Well, if he did, he'd probably leave it at the cash desk downstairs. Go down, Steve – buy some biscuits or cakes or something and –
STEVE:	If I can get them!
TEMPLE:	– and make a sort of casual enquiry. Don't seem too concerned about it.

The orchestra starts to play again.

STEVE:	I know, darling!
FORBES:	The name's Bennett, Steve.
STEVE:	(*Going*) Yes. I shan't be long.

CUT TO: The Café Cash Desk.

In the background, the café door is heard opening and closing, and a few people are passing to and fro. We hear the sound of a cash-register.

STEVE:	Could I have some of those cakes, please?
WAITRESS:	I'm sorry, madam, they're for the café only.
STEVE:	Well, have you any biscuits?
WAITRESS:	I'm afraid we haven't any sweet – oh, excuse me – Good afternoon, Mrs Forester!
MRS FORESTER:	Good afternoon.
WAITRESS:	Your parcel's ready for you, Madam.
MRS FORESTER:	Oh, thank you.

The WAITRESS hands over the parcel.

WAITRESS: Are you staying down here for long this time, Mrs Forester?

MRS FORESTER: Oh, I really don't know – perhaps a week or ten days – rather depends on the weather. (*Taking the parcel*) Thank you. Will you put that down to me?

WAITRESS: Of course.

MRS FORESTER: (*Going*) Good afternoon.

WAITRESS: Good afternoon, Madam.

The café door opens and closes in the background as MRS FORESTER leaves.

WAITRESS: Now, you wanted some biscuits?

STEVE: Please. (*Casually*) Does that lady live near here?

WAITRESS: Mrs Forester?

STEVE: Yes.

WAITRESS: She has a house outside Greenchurch on the Willesborough Road. It's a lovely place – you must have seen it – Camberley Lodge.

STEVE: Oh, yes! I believe my husband pointed it out to me on the way down from Town.

The WAITRESS opens a tin.

WAITRESS: Will these be all right, Madam? I'm afraid they're the only biscuits we have left.

STEVE: Yes, they'll do nicely, thank you. Oh, by the way, we expected to meet a friend of ours here – a Mr Bennett. I don't know whether he left a message or not?

WAITRESS: I don't think so, Madam.

STEVE: Oh, well, it doesn't matter. How much is that?

Start to FADE SCENE.

WAITRESS: One and a penny, please!

STEVE: Thank you.

WAITRESS: And your ration book …

STEVE: Oh, yes; I was forgetting all about the book!

CUT TO: Upstairs at the Britannia Café, Greenchurch, as before.

The orchestra is playing.

TEMPLE: … I don't see any reason for being suspicious, Sir Graham, but the fact remains, Braddock must have discovered something otherwise he would never have sent that telegram.

FORBES: Mmm …

TEMPLE: Oh, here's Steve, and she looks pretty excited about something …

The orchestra stops and there is a smattering of applause.

FORBES: Hello, Steve – any luck?

TEMPLE: What's happened?

STEVE: Braddock didn't leave a message, but …

TEMPLE: Yes?

STEVE: You know that woman, darling – Mrs Forester?

FORBES: Yes. What about her?

STEVE: She's got a house down here – just outside Greenchurch. A place called Camberley Lodge.

TEMPLE: (*Extremely interested*) She has, has she?

STEVE: She was downstairs just now, I nearly bumped into her.

FORBES:	(*Thoughtfully*) I wonder if that's what Braddock discovered?
TEMPLE:	We'll go back to the inn. If there's no sign of Braddock by nine o'clock, we'll call on Mrs Forester.

Play Incidental Music.

CUT TO: Inside the TEMPLES' Car.

The car is starting to slow down.

FORBES:	We can't have much further to go now.
TEMPLE:	No. Sir Graham, are you coming up to the house with us or staying in the car?
FORBES:	As it's a social call I think I'd better stay in the car, Temple.
TEMPLE:	All right.
STEVE:	Here we are, darling!
FORBES:	That must be the place over on the left.
TEMPLE:	We'll park the car here and walk up the drive.

The car slows down to a standstill.

TEMPLE:	Give us a quarter of an hour, Sir Graham, then if you don't hear from us –
FORBES:	I'll storm the Bastille!
TEMPLE:	(*Laughing*) Yes.

TEMPLE switches the engine off.

TEMPLE:	Right, Steve?
STEVE:	Yes.

TEMPLE opens his door.

TEMPLE:	It'll take us about three or four minutes to get up the drive – you'd better make it twenty minutes, Sir Graham.
FORBES:	All right, Temple.
TEMPLE:	Come along, Steve!

CUT TO: The Drive.

TEMPLE and STEVE are walking up the gravel drive. It is late evening.

STEVE: We should be near the house by now, surely.

TEMPLE: I think it's just round the next bend.

STEVE: It's much darker than I thought it would be.

TEMPLE: It's all these trees and bushes ... Listen!

STEVE: What is it?

TEMPLE: Ssh!

STEVE: I don't hear anything.

TEMPLE: Ssh!

Suddenly, from the background, we hear the cry of an owl.

STEVE: Sounds like an owl or something.

TEMPLE: Maybe.

STEVE gives a quick, nervous, shudder.

TEMPLE: Are you cold, Steve?

STEVE: No, it's not that, darling.

TEMPLE: Nervous?

STEVE: Well – not exactly nervous, but ...

TEMPLE: I know.

TEMPLE and STEVE continue to walk along the drive.

STEVE: Paul?

TEMPLE: Yes?

STEVE: I've been thinking about this business; and you know, there's something I don't quite understand.

TEMPLE: There's a great deal I don't understand, Steve. For one thing, if that taxi-driver, the poor devil that was shot, intended to take us ... (*He is listening*) ... to Abel Dunne's then ...

STEVE: ... Paul, what is it?

TEMPLE: That isn't an owl, Steve. I'm sure it isn't.

STEVE: What?

TEMPLE: Don't you hear it?

STEVE: No.
TEMPLE: Darling, listen.
There is complete silence.
STEVE: Paul, there isn't anything … Honestly dear, I –
TEMPLE: Steve, listen!
Silence. Then in the distant background we hear a low soft cry; almost a whispered moan.
STEVE: What was that?
TEMPLE: Now do you hear it?
The cry is heard again.
TEMPLE: Do you hear it?
STEVE: Yes …
The cry is heard again.
STEVE: Paul – Paul, what is it?

END OF EPISODE FIVE

EPISODE SIX

STEVE'S INTUITION

OPEN TO:

ANNOUNCER: Paul Temple, the celebrated novelist and private detective, is visited by Sir Graham Forbes of Scotland Yard and by Mr Philip Kaufman who is attached to the Special Branch. Kaufman tells Paul Temple about a notorious criminal known as Dr Belasco. Temple promises to try and discover the identity of Belasco and during the course of certain investigations makes the acquaintance of Henry Worth, David Nelson, Mrs Forester, Joseph – a servant of Mrs Forester's – and a certain Mr Ed Bellamy. Late one night, Temple and Steve – together with Sir Graham Forbes – visit Camberley Lodge, which is a large country house owned by Mrs Forester. Sir Graham remains in the car whilst Temple and Steve proceed towards the house on foot.

CUT TO: The Gravel Drive of Camberley Lodge. Night.

STEVE: ... Paul, what is it?

TEMPLE: That isn't an owl, Steve. I'm sure it isn't.

STEVE: What?

TEMPLE: Don't you hear it?

STEVE: No.

TEMPLE: Darling, listen.

Faintly, in the distant background we can hear a low soft cry; almost a whispered moan.

STEVE: What was that?

TEMPLE: Now do you hear it?

STEVE: Yes – what is it?

The cry is heard again.

STEVE: Paul, what is it?

TEMPLE: I don't know … Come on, Steve! Let's go up to the house!

CUT TO: By the front door of the house.

TEMPLE and STEVE approach over the gravel.

TEMPLE: (*Surprised*) The door's open …

STEVE: Yes … but don't go in without –

TEMPLE: Listen!

A moment: in the background we can hear the same, low moan. It is a little nearer.

TEMPLE: Did you hear it?

STEVE: Yes – where's it coming from?

TEMPLE: I don't know, but it's certainly not coming from the house.

STEVE: It sounds to me as if it's coming from over the other side – near those bushes.

TEMPLE takes a step forward and examines the steps.

TEMPLE: M'm.

STEVE: What are you doing?

TEMPLE: I'm just looking at the step, darling …

STEVE takes a step forward.

STEVE: It's blood!

TEMPLE: Yes.

STEVE: Paul, what do you think's happened?

Footsteps are heard approaching.

TEMPLE: Sh! Sh! There's someone coming!

STEVE: Who is it?

It is MRS FORESTER and JOSEPH. They are talking together in a quiet, friendly manner. Suddenly, their footsteps stop, and they stop talking. They have realised that there is someone waiting at the entrance to the house.

MRS FORESTER: Who is it, Joseph?

JOSEPH: (*Calling*) Hello? Who is that?

TEMPLE: Good evening, Mrs Forester!

MRS FORESTER: Why – it's Mr Temple!

MRS FORESTER and JOSEPH arrive at the house.

MRS FORESTER: Well, this is a surprise! (*A friendly laugh*) What on earth are you doing down here?

TEMPLE: I came down to see a friend of mine – or rather – an acquaintance. (*Watching MRS FORESTER*) A Mr Bennett.

MRS FORESTER: Bennett?

TEMPLE: Yes, he's staying at the Cromwell Heart. Quite by chance I heard that you'd got a house down here so – Oh, I beg your pardon! This is my wife.

MRS FORESTER: How do you do. (*Suddenly, remembering*) Weren't – weren't you in the café this afternoon?

STEVE: (*Laughing*) Yes.

MRS FORESTER: (*Amused*) No doubt that's how you discovered …

JOSEPH: (*Quietly interrupting MRS FORESTER*) Mrs Forester …

MRS FORESTER: Yes, what is it, Joseph?

JOSEPH: The door, Madam.

MRS FORESTER: What about the – why, it's open! Did you open the door, Mr Temple?

TEMPLE: No.

MRS FORESTER: But … Joseph, what is it?

JOSEPH: Look at the step. Look – there's blood on it …

MRS FORESTER gives a quick, startled gasp.

MRS FORESTER: How long have you been here?

TEMPLE: About two minutes.

MRS FORESTER: Was the door open when you arrived?

TEMPLE: I've already told you I didn't open the door, Mrs Forester.

MRS FORESTER: But … I don't understand, … I'm quite sure that we didn't leave the door open and yet … Joseph! Go into the house and see that everything's all right!

TEMPLE: (*Rather surprised*) Aren't there any other servants in the house?

MRS FORESTER: No. Apart from Joseph I only employ a man and his wife and a girl of sixteen, and they're spending the evening at Willesborough. They won't get back until much later. Go along, Joseph!

TEMPLE: Would you like me to come with you?

JOSEPH: Well – if you wouldn't mind, sir.

TEMPLE: (*Going*) Come along! (*To STEVE*) We shan't be long.

TEMPLE and JOSEPH go into the house.

MRS FORESTER: This is all rather bewildering.

STEVE: Have you been away from the house for long?

MRS FORESTER: What do you mean? Oh, I see … About half an hour, I should say. We walked down to a cottage of mine – it's about half a mile from the main gate.

STEVE: Oh, yes – I believe I noticed it. It's a rather pretty little cottage with a thatched roof.

MRS FORESTER: That's right. It's occupied by an old man called Bert Travis. He used to work on the estate – oh, donkey's years ago when my father owned the place.

STEVE: After you left him – you came straight back here?

MRS FORESTER: Why yes, of course.

STEVE: That must have been about ten or fifteen minutes ago?

MRS FORESTER: Possibly a little longer.

STEVE: I suppose Mr Travis could verify that?

MRS FORESTER: Of course, he could verify it – if you consider it necessary, Mrs Temple.

STEVE: I've got a feeling that it may be necessary, Mrs Forester.

MRS FORESTER: What do you mean –?

JOSEPH and TEMPLE return.

JOSEPH: Mrs Forester …

MRS FORESTER: What's happened?

JOSEPH: There's someone in the shrubbery … Mr Temple drew back the curtains in the lounge and we could see him.

STEVE: Paul?

TEMPLE: There's someone at the back of the house. It rather looks as if the poor devil's been knocked out.

STEVE: That must have been the noise we heard! He must have been trying to shout for help.

JOSEPH: Mr Temple – This blood on the step …

TEMPLE: (*Watching JOSEPH*) Yes, Joseph?

JOSEPH: Well – it looks as if whoever was hurt – must have been taken through the front door and out of the house.

MRS FORESTER: But that's impossible. Quite impossible.

TEMPLE: Why is it impossible?

MRS FORESTER: Well …

149

TEMPLE: Did you take anyone out of the house tonight, Mrs Forester?

MRS FORESTER: No! Of course, we didn't! Did we, Joseph?

JOSEPH: Why, no, Madam!

A moment.

TEMPLE: All right. Come along, Joseph, let's go round to the back of the house. Steve, stay with Mrs Forester, please.

CUT TO: The Shrubbery.

JOSEPH and TEMPLE are forcing their way through the branches and leaves.

JOSEPH: The window's over on the left, sir.

TEMPLE: Where? Oh, yes, I see. Well – we want to be a little more this way, I think.

JOSEPH: Yes, sir. There's a hedge just over on the right. Mind your face on that branch, sir … Look! Look, sir!

TEMPLE: Yes, I see him.

TEMPLE and JOSEPH move further into the shrubbery.

JOSEPH: Oh, horrible!

TEMPLE: Oh Lord.

JOSEPH: What's happened to him?

TEMPLE: Obviously, he's been beaten up by someone and then apparently dragged here.

JOSEPH: Is he dead?

TEMPLE: Yes.

JOSEPH: Who is he, sir – (*A tiny pause*) – do you know?

TEMPLE: His name's Braddock.

Play Incidental Music.

CUT TO: SIR GRAHAM's Office at Scotland Yard.

TEMPLE: I still maintain, Sir Graham, that until you find Abel Dunne, or the lorry for that matter, you can't possibly justify that statement –

FORBES: (*Interrupting TEMPLE*) Don't let's confuse the issue, Temple! I sent Braddock down to Greenchurch because I was under the impression that Dunne had taken the lorry there and was going to contact Belasco. Now Braddock must have discovered something: something of supreme importance.

TEMPLE: Otherwise he wouldn't have been murdered.

FORBES: Exactly.

TEMPLE: And what do you think he discovered?

FORBES: Isn't it obvious? He discovered that Mrs Forester was Dr Belasco!

TEMPLE: But you've had your men down there for two days, you've been over the district with a tooth-comb, and you still haven't found any sign of the lorry or the elusive Mr Dunne.

FORBES: Nevertheless, I still think the lorry's down there.

TEMPLE: What do you think, Kaufman?

KAUFMAN: I'm still suspicious of our friend Mr Worth, but at the moment I must confess I'm strongly inclined to agree with Sir Graham. After all, this isn't one of your detective novels.

TEMPLE: What do you mean?

KAUFMAN:	Well – just because Mrs Forester appears to be so obviously guilty it doesn't necessarily mean that she's innocent.
TEMPLE:	In other words, you agree with Sir Graham?
KAUFMAN:	I do!
FORBES:	Well, whether you agree or not, I've taken the necessary steps.
TEMPLE:	What steps?
FORBES:	I've sent Perry down to Greenchurch – he went down first thing this morning. I've arrested Mrs Forester for the murder of Norman Braddock.
TEMPLE:	For the murder of Braddock?
FORBES:	Good heavens, Temple, you're not going to tell me she didn't murder Braddock?
KAUFMAN:	She murdered Braddock, I'm certain of that.
TEMPLE:	What makes you so certain, Mr Kaufman?
KAUFMAN:	But it is so obvious!
FORBES:	I agree.
KAUFMAN:	Look! As soon as he arrives at Greenchurch, Braddock discovers that Mrs Forester is living in the district. He makes discreet enquiries, and then one day – the day after you and Sir Graham decide to go down there – he suddenly decides to visit the house – what do you call it – Camberley Lodge. He is discovered searching the house – presumably by Mrs Forester and Joseph. He is beaten up –
TEMPLE:	By Mrs Forester?
KAUFMAN:	Well – by the two of them. Then, when it is dark, they take him outside and dump

152

	him in the shrubbery. It's my contention that they were actually doing this when you and Mrs Temple arrived at the house.
TEMPLE:	M'm.
KAUFMAN:	But don't you see? It fits together. It fits together like a jig-saw puzzle! For instance, when you and Mrs Temple arrived at the house the door was open. Now, if Mrs Forester and Joseph were just at the back of the house – as I suspect – then they'd leave the door open, it would be more or less a natural thing to do.
TEMPLE:	Yes, but just a minute, Kaufman! We checked the alibi. They really did visit the cottage.
KAUFMAN:	Maybe so, but that doesn't necessarily prove anything.
TEMPLE:	Well, I've got an alternative theory, and incidentally one which I have expounded before, Sir Graham, under rather similar circumstances.
FORBES:	The Reyburn case?
TEMPLE:	Yes. Now, supposing Braddock was murdered – not by Mrs Forester or Joseph – but by someone else. Someone who wanted to throw suspicion – or shall we say continue to throw suspicion – on to Mrs Forester?
KAUFMAN:	I'm listening.
TEMPLE:	And supposing that person deliberately took Braddock down to Camberley Lodge?
FORBES:	Go on.

TEMPLE:	When they arrived at the house it was empty, Mrs Forester and Joseph being at the cottage.
KAUFMAN:	Well?
TEMPLE:	Well, supposing that person opened the front door with a pass key and dumped Braddock in the hall.
KAUFMAN:	But he wasn't found in the hall, he was found in the shrubbery!
TEMPLE:	Of course, he was!
KAUFMAN:	What do you mean?
TEMPLE:	I mean that when Braddock was left at Camberley Lodge, he wasn't dead! He got up, opened the front door, instinctively left it open, and then staggered out on to the drive. It was getting dark, the poor devil was frightened. He made his way round to the back of the house – and collapsed in the shrubbery.
KAUFMAN:	And you expect us to believe, Mr Temple, that the person that murdered Braddock –
TEMPLE:	Dr Belasco.
KAUFMAN:	(*Nodding*) Dr Belasco. You expect us to believe that Dr Belasco – by sheer coincidence – had a pass key to Mrs Forester's house? That's stretching the imagination too far, my friend. No! It was Mrs Forester, assisted by Joseph, who murdered Braddock. I'm absolutely certain of that.
TEMPLE:	(*Lightly*) Well, I'm delighted to hear you say so, Kaufman. There's nothing I like better than to hear a man say he's absolutely convinced about something! So,

154

Mrs Forester, aided and abetted by the amiable Joseph, murders Braddock and – instead of taking him for a nice long ride – dumps him, more or less, on her own front doorstep.

There is a quick knock, and the door opens.

FORBES: What is it, Sergeant?

SERGEANT: I beg your pardon, sir, but a Mr Bellamy's called, sir. He'd rather like a word with Mr Temple.

FORBES: Bellamy?

SERGEANT: Yes, sir. A Mr Ed Bellamy.

KAUFMAN: Isn't that the man at the Machicha Club?

TEMPLE: Yes.

FORBES: Have you any idea what he wants, Temple?

TEMPLE: I haven't the slightest idea.

FORBES: M'm. Ask him in, Sergeant.

SERGEANT: (*Going*) Very good, sir.

FORBES: Bellamy …? (*He snaps his fingers*) Oh, yes, of course! The car accident – Steve and David Nelson.

SERGEANT: (*Returning*) Mr Bellamy, sir.

The SERGEANT ushers BELLAMY in, then leaves, closing the door.

FORBES: Come in, Mr Bellamy.

BELLAMY: Oh thanks! Ah, hello, Temple!

TEMPLE: Hello, Bellamy – what can I do for you?

BELLAMY: Well – I telephoned your flat, and your wife told me that you were at Scotland Yard, so … Well, I guess that kind of … sort of made up my mind for me.

FORBES: What do you mean?

155

BELLAMY: I've been trying to make up my mind to
                come and see you for the last twelve
                hours, Sir Graham, but … well …

TEMPLE: You thought you'd compromise by seeing
                me?

BELLAMY: Yeah – that's just about it.

FORBES: What did you want to see Mr Temple
                about?

BELLAMY: Well – Now look. Let's get this straight. I
                don't like a guy who goes around shooting
                his mouth. There are times when – well –
                it kind of pays to talk first and think
                afterwards.

TEMPLE: What's on your mind, Mr Bellamy?

BELLAMY: May I sit down?

FORBES: Yes, of course.

BELLAMY sits.

BELLAMY: Last night, at about a quarter past eight, I
                was – Sorry, just a moment. Who's this?

KAUFMAN: My name is Kaufman.

FORBES: Mr Kaufman is attached to the Special
                Branch.

BELLAMY: Kaufman? Oh, yeah! Yeah, I remember
                now. You came to the club one night about
                three weeks ago.

KAUFMAN: Did I?

BELLAMY: Sure. You danced with a tall, blonde rather
                good-looking girl.

KAUFMAN: You appear to have an excellent memory,
                Mr Bellamy.

BELLAMY: I get by.

TEMPLE: You were saying?

BELLAMY: Oh, yeah. Last night, somewhere round
                about quarter past eight. I was in the club,

156

strolling around, saying hello to the folks, having a few drinks – you know how it is. When suddenly one of the waiters came up to me.

CUT TO: The Machicha Club.

We hear the dance orchestra and a vocalist. The number is a gay, sophisticated one. There is general laughter and gaiety. ANDROS the waiter is Greek. He is a man of about 60.

ANDROS: Excuse me, Mr Bellamy.
BELLAMY: Yes, Andros – what is it?
ANDROS: Are you expecting anyone, sir?
BELLAMY: Expecting anyone? What do you mean?
ANDROS: There's a young gentleman, sir – he … he went upstairs into your office – a few moments ago.
BELLAMY: Into my office?
ANDROS: Yes, sir.
BELLAMY: (*A little laugh*) You must be mistaken.
ANDROS: No, sir, I watched him most particularly, he walked up the stairs, straight into the office.

After a moment.

BELLAMY: Do you know Inspector Perry?
ANDROS: It was not Inspector Perry, sir.
BELLAMY: You're sure?
ANDROS: I'm quite sure, sir.
BELLAMY: Yes, O.K., Andros.
ANDROS: Thank you, sir.

The dance orchestra and restaurant noises continue.
Very SLOW FADE, terminating with:

CUT TO: BELLAMY's Office at the Club.

The door opens. BELLAMY enters and closes the door. Dead silence.

BELLAMY: I don't know whether you know it or not, brother, that's my desk you're sitting at.

WORTH is completely self-possessed. He is infinitely more sure of himself than in any preceding scene.

WORTH: It's an extremely nice desk, Mr Bellamy. You are a man after my own heart.

BELLAMY: What do you mean?

WORTH: I am referring to your impeccable taste. This office, for instance.

BELLAMY: What's the matter with it?

WORTH: There's nothing the matter with it. Always providing, of course, that you like this sort of thing.

BELLAMY: Listen, brother, when I go in for small talk it's usually with dames! Now what's this all about?

WORTH: Your partner in this business, the late Mr –

BELLAMY: Partner? I've got no partner – I've never had a partner!

WORTH: I am referring to the late Mr Harry Marx.

BELLAMY: Marx invested £12,000 in this place, but that didn't make him a partner.

WORTH: No?

BELLAMY: No!

WORTH: Oh, you surprise me, Mr Bellamy.

BELLAMY: I'm thinking you'll get a lot more surprises before we're through!

WORTH: However, shall we continue? Your partner – (*Corrects himself*) – your associate, the late Mr Harry Marx, entered into negotiations with a certain Dr Belasco.

158

BELLAMY:	(*Quietly*) Dr Belasco?
WORTH:	Yes.
BELLAMY:	What sort of negotiations?
WORTH:	It was agreed that Marx – or rather you – or shall we say the Machicha Club?
BELLAMY:	Say what you like – but get to the point!
WORTH:	It was agreed that the Machicha Club would purchase certain commodities from Dr Belasco, commodities which could not be readily obtained in the – legitimate market.
BELLAMY:	(*Down to earth*) What are you selling?

A pause.

WORTH:	At the moment, cigarettes.
BELLAMY:	(*Laughing*) Cigarettes! Who the – (*Suddenly: it dawning on him*) Say, I read about that! £17,000 worth, eh? This guy Belasco's got plenty of nerve!
WORTH:	(*Unperturbed*) Mr Bellamy.
BELLAMY:	Yes?
WORTH:	Take this piece of paper.
BELLAMY:	What is it?
WORTH:	Take it.

BELLAMY takes it and reads.

BELLAMY:	"Kennington Cottage, Reiford, Kent" … What is this?
WORTH:	You are requested to bring £900 – in cash – to that address tomorrow night. Be there by 10 o'clock – certainly not later than 10.15. You understand?
BELLAMY:	£900! Are you crazy?
WORTH:	Arrangements will be made for the delivery of the cigarettes as soon as the money –

BELLAMY: Now just a minute! You listen to me, my
                fancy friend! You tell this Dr – Dr
                Livingstone or whatever the hell they call
                the guy that I give the orders around here,
                and Harry Marx or nobody else was in a
                position to negotiate a deal without my
                consent. When I want cigarettes, or
                whisky, or any other God-darn thing I
                know where to get it, without contacting
                Dr Belasco!

A moment.

WORTH: Mr Bellamy.
BELLAMY: Yeah?
WORTH: No doubt you heard about the Silver Club?
BELLAMY: Of course, I heard! It was in the papers.
                They had a fire and the whole place was
                burnt down to the – (*He stops*)

A pause.

WORTH: A most regrettable incident.
BELLAMY: Are you threatening me, Mr -?
WORTH: Worth. Henry Worth.
BELLAMY: Are you threatening me, Mr Worth,
                because by heck if you are –
WORTH: I am purely suggesting that you do
                precisely as you are told. £900. 10 o'clock
                tomorrow night. The address is on the
                piece of paper, Mr Bellamy.

CUT TO: SIR GRAHAM's Office at Scotland Yard, as
before.

BELLAMY: … Well, I didn't quite know what to do
                about it. Then suddenly it occurred to me
                that the most sensible thing to do was to
                go along and have a chat with Mr Temple.

160

KAUFMAN: Surely the most obvious thing to do was to come straight to Scotland Yard.

BELLAMY: (*Good-natured*) I never do the most obvious thing, Mr Kaufman – on principle.

FORBES: Have you the piece of paper he gave you?

BELLAMY passes over the paper.

BELLAMY: Here it is. It won't tell you much, I'm afraid; it's typed.

FORBES: (*Reading*) "Kennington Cottage, Reiford, Kent." M'm.

TEMPLE: Bellamy, you say that Worth was very self-possessed – extremely sure of himself, in fact.

BELLAMY: Extremely.

TEMPLE: Did he give you the impression that he – himself – was Dr Belasco?

BELLAMY: I don't know. No. No, I don't think he did. As a matter of fact, I don't quite know why, but I rather got the impression that Dr Belasco was a woman.

TEMPLE: What gave you that impression?

BELLAMY: I don't know. You know how it is. A person talks – they say something in a particular way – they make a certain kind of gesture. Well, it isn't so much what they say, as how they say it.

FORBES: I know what you mean. And I think you're right, Bellamy. I think Dr Belasco is a woman, and I think that woman is Mrs Forester.

BELLAMY: Mrs Forester?

TEMPLE: (*Quietly*) Yes, Mr Bellamy.

BELLAMY: (*Turning*) Yes?

TEMPLE: Supposing I suggested that Worth deliberately went out of his way to convey the impression that Dr Belasco was a woman. How would that strike you?

BELLAMY: Well – it seems to me that if that was at the back of his mind, he'd have played it up a bit more. You know what I mean: subtle, but mysterious references to the little lady behind the scenes.

TEMPLE: Don't you think that would have been a little too obvious?

BELLAMY: Well, maybe – maybe?

FORBES: You haven't said anything to anyone else about this?

BELLAMY: Not a word.

FORBES: Right, Bellamy! We'll pick you up tonight at the Club shortly after 8 o'clock, and I advise you to –

BELLAMY: What do you mean, pick me up? … You want me to keep that appointment, is that it?

FORBES: That's it, Mr Bellamy.

BELLAMY: But surely –

BELLAMY is interrupted by the sudden opening of the door.

FORBES: Why, hello, Perry.

PERRY: Good morning, Sir Graham.

FORBES: You've been quick, Perry, I never dreamt that – (*He stops*)

KAUFMAN: What is it? Is something the matter?

PERRY: Yes.

FORBES: Well, what is it? Speak up, man!

PERRY: Mrs Forester and Joseph left Greenchurh by car shortly after seven o'clock this

	morning. Just outside Maidstone the car skidded and …
FORBES:	And what?
PERRY:	Joseph escaped with a mere shaking – it was nothing short of a miracle.
FORBES:	And Mrs Forester?
PERRY:	Mrs Forester is dead.
FORBES:	Dead?
KAUFMAN:	But this is ridiculous!
FORBES:	Who identified the body?
PERRY:	I did, Sir Graham.

Play Incidental Music.

CUT TO: A Police Car.

The car is travelling fast: INSPECTOR PERRY is driving. It is an extremely stormy night: rain, wind and a distant background of thunder can be heard.

BELLAMY:	What a night.
FORBES:	It's simply teeming down.
TEMPLE:	Can you see all right, Inspector?
PERRY:	(*Peering out*) It's not … It's not too bad.
BELLAMY:	Did you check up on this place?
FORBES:	Yes, we checked up on it.
BELLAMY:	Well, how far is it?
FORBES:	It's about four miles the other side of Staplehurst.
BELLAMY:	Well, the sooner we get there the better.
TEMPLE:	Nervous, Mr Bellamy?
BELLAMY:	Nervous? I'm like a jelly in a high wind!
FORBES:	There's no need to be nervous, just play the whole thing perfectly straight.
BELLAMY:	I don't know. I don't trust these guys.

TEMPLE:	All you've got to do is to deliver the money and convey the impression that you intend to do exactly as you're told.
BELLAMY:	I'm not very good at conveying that sort of impression.
TEMPLE:	Don't worry, you'll get by all right.

A pause.

PERRY:	We're coming into Staplehurst, sir.
FORBES:	Yes. You'd better take over, Bellamy, when we get through Staplehurst.
BELLAMY:	Yes, O.K.

There is a roll of thunder and heavy rain beats against the car.

PERRY:	This is what I call real movie weather.
FORBES:	What do you mean?
PERRY:	Well, when it rains on the pictures it's usually like this. It never rains but it pours!

They laugh.

BELLAMY:	Sir Graham?
FORBES:	Yes?
BELLAMY:	(*Hesitating*) You don't think that, now Mrs Forester is dead, we're on a wild goose chase?
FORBES:	No, I don't. I'm convinced that Mrs Forester was Dr Belasco – but I'm equally convinced that someone'll turn up at the cottage. And I've got a shrewd idea that that … (*The car slows down*) What is it, Perry?
PERRY:	I think we turn here, sir.
BELLAMY:	Yes, there's the signpost. You turn to the left.
PERRY:	Ah, yes, I see.

FORBES: Slow down, Inspector. Eh, you'd better
             take over now, Bellamy.

BELLAMY: Yes, O.K.

PERRY slows down the car.

PERRY: Shall I stay in the front of the car, sir?

FORBES: No. You'd better sit at the back with us,
             Perry; and keep well down just in case
             they've planted a lookout on one of the
             roads.

CUT TO: The Police Car.   A Short While Later.

BELLAMY is now driving as they approach the cottage.
The rain is not quite so heavy.

TEMPLE: Here we are, Sir Graham!

The car slows down to a standstill.

BELLAMY: There's someone there – there's a light in
             the cottage!

BELLAMY switches the car engine off.

FORBES: Yes. Now you know what to do, Bellamy.
             Just keep your nerve and play the whole
             thing perfectly straight.

TEMPLE: Don't be too easy going or they'll be
             suspicious, be tough but – well – give in.

BELLAMY: O.K. I'll do the best I can!

BELLAMY opens the car door and starts to get out.

TEMPLE: I shouldn't forget the briefcase, Mr
             Bellamy.

BELLAMY: (*Turning*) What? Oh! Gee, I mustn't forget
             that!

TEMPLE: Good luck!

BELLAMY: Thanks.

BELLAMY picks up the briefcase, gets out of the car and
shuts the door.
A pause.

165

FORBES: Can you see him?

TEMPLE: Yes … He's nearly at the cottage.

PERRY: I'll get out and wipe the windscreen and then we'll be able to –

FORBES: No! Don't get out of the car, Perry, just in case there's anyone watching.

PERRY: Sir.

A revolver shot is heard in the distance.

FORBES: Now where the devil did that come from?

PERRY: It came from the cottage!

FORBES: Yes!

TEMPLE: Bellamy must have heard it, and –

PERRY: Yes. Look, he's running up to the cottage. (*Surprised*) Hello!

TEMPLE: He's looking through the window.

PERRY: What's he doing? … He's waving to us!

FORBES: I don't think he is.

PERRY: Yes, he is, sir!

TEMPLE: Yes, he is. He must have seen something through the window.

PERRY: He's waving again – he wants us to go over there!

TEMPLE: He's gone into the cottage. Get in the front, Inspector! Be quick! Start the car! Let's get over there!

Play Incidental Music.

CUT TO: Outside the Cottage.

The police car draws up, doors open as TEMPLE, FORBES and PERRY get out as BELLAMY approaches.

TEMPLE: There's Bellamy! Coming out of the cottage!

FORBES: What happened, Bellamy?

BELLAMY: (*Out of breath*) Did you hear that shot?

TEMPLE: Yes.

BELLAMY: I was about twenty yards from the cottage when I heard it. I realised that it had come from the cottage and I …

TEMPLE: You ran over to the window. Yes, we saw you!

BELLAMY: There's a man. I … I don't know who he is. He's been shot. He's in the kitchen.

TEMPLE: Come along, Sir Graham!

CUT TO: The Cottage Kitchen

INSPECTOR PERRY is going through the dead man's possessions.

PERRY: A watch … a wallet … identification card. M'm – it's the laddie we've been looking for all right. It's Abel Dunne.

FORBES: But what happened? He obviously came here to meet Bellamy; surely if he'd intended to commit suicide –

PERRY: Suicide!

TEMPLE: He didn't commit suicide, Sir Graham.

BELLAMY: Just a minute! This suicide idea isn't as crazy as it sounds. Supposing he guessed that you were here – the police, I mean – he got the breeze up and decided … No, no, I guess that doesn't make sense. No, he'd make a run for it.

TEMPLE: What exactly happened, Bellamy?

BELLAMY: Well, I guess you saw what happened. I was about twenty yards away from the cottage, I heard the revolver shot and I dashed up to the window.

TEMPLE: You saw Dunne sprawled across the table?

BELLAMY: I saw him exactly as he is now.

167

TEMPLE: Did you see anyone else?

BELLAMY: Not a soul. As soon as I saw what had happened I … I waved to you and … and dashed into the cottage.

FORBES: You didn't see anyone else – in the cottage, I mean?

BELLAMY: No. I heard a door bang at the back and I … I ran out there – but I certainly didn't see anybody.

TEMPLE: Of course, it's fairly dark …

BELLAMY: It's dark all right, but I should have thought if there'd been anybody around, I would have spotted them.

FORBES: Yes, I'm inclined to agree – (*He stops*)

The sound of a car drawing up to the cottage is heard.

TEMPLE: Who's this?

FORBES: Can you see, Inspector?

The car door opens and closes.

PERRY: (*Peering through the window*) It's Mr Kaufman!

FORBES: Kaufman?

TEMPLE: I thought you told Kaufman to wait for us at Yalding?

FORBES: I did.

The door opens and KAUFMAN enters.

TEMPLE: Hello, Kaufman.

KAUFMAN: Hello, Temple.

FORBES: I thought I told you to wait for us at Yalding?

KAUFMAN: I got rather worried, Sir Graham. I began to wonder what exactly was going on … (*He sees the body*) Who is this?

TEMPLE: His name is Dunne.

KAUFMAN: Abel Dunne?

TEMPLE: Yes.
KAUFMAN: (*Impressed*) So!
TEMPLE: Kaufman …
KAUFMAN: Yes?
TEMPLE: Have you been here before – this evening?
KAUFMAN: Why – why, no! Of course not! Why do you ask?
TEMPLE: I wondered, that's all.

CUT TO: The TEMPLES' Hall.
The sound of a key in a lock is heard, the door opens, and TEMPLE enters.
STEVE: Hello, darling! You're not as late as I expected.
TEMPLE closes the door.
TEMPLE: No, we – M'm, is that coffee I can smell?
STEVE: Yes.
TEMPLE: Smells delicious!
STEVE: Come along, let's go into the lounge. (*Calling*) Charlie, we'll have the coffee in the lounge!
CHARLIE: (*From the kitchen*) Okedoke!
TEMPLE: I do wish he wouldn't say "okedoke"!
STEVE laughs.

CUT TO: The TEMPLES' Lounge.
TEMPLE and STEVE are drinking their coffee.
STEVE: How did you know it was Abel Dunne?
TEMPLE: He had a wallet with several letters in it. Oh, it was Dunne all right.
A moment.
STEVE: Paul?
TEMPLE: Yes, darling?

STEVE: Do you really think this means the end of the Belasco affair?

TEMPLE: What do you mean?

STEVE: Well, if Sir Graham's right and Mrs Forester was Dr Belasco, then the whole business is finished.

TEMPLE: Do you think Mrs Forester was Dr Belasco?

STEVE: I don't know. Everything points towards it and yet …

TEMPLE: Well?

STEVE: Paul …

TEMPLE: Yes, Steve?

STEVE: If I say something which sounds utterly and completely absurd you won't think me mad?

TEMPLE: No.

STEVE: Well – I've got a sort of intuition.

TEMPLE: What, again!

STEVE: Now don't you laugh. I was right about Edward Day and the Gregory Affair.

TEMPLE: Well, who do you suspect this time – Charlie?

STEVE: You're the one that should suspect Charlie, darling.

TEMPLE: (*Laughs, then suddenly sees the point*) Here, what do you mean?

STEVE: No, seriously, I've got the strangest sort of feeling about –

TEMPLE: Kaufman?

STEVE: Yes! Why – what makes you say that?

TEMPLE: Kaufman's got a pretty good record you know, Steve. To all intents and purposes there doesn't appear to be the slightest justification for suspecting Kaufman.

STEVE: To all intents and purposes?

TEMPLE: I said that because – Hello! Is this tonight's paper?

TEMPLE picks up a newspaper from the settee.

STEVE: Yes. They've got the Forester story on the front page.

TEMPLE: So I see. It's not a very good photograph of her, is it?

STEVE: I didn't think it was too bad. After all, newspaper photographs are never very good –

STEVE breaks off as the door is suddenly thrown open.

CHARLIE: I beg your pardon, m'm, but we've got a visitor.

STEVE: Charlie! At this hour?

TEMPLE: Who on earth could – Good heavens, Mr Nelson!

STEVE: What's the meaning of this, Mr Nelson?

NELSON: (*Perturbed and excited*) I'm sorry to crash in like this, Mrs Temple, it's quite unforgiveable I know, but – well …

TEMPLE: That's all right, Charlie – you may go.

CHARLIE leaves, closing the door.

TEMPLE: Now – what is it?

NELSON: You've seen tonight's papers?

TEMPLE: Yes.

NELSON: About Mrs Forester, I mean – about her being dead?

TEMPLE: Of course.

NELSON: Well, that's just the point!

STEVE: What do you mean?

NELSON: She's not dead!

STEVE: Not dead?

NELSON: I saw her myself half an hour ago!

END OF EPISODE SIX

EPISODE SEVEN

THE SUSPECTS

OPEN TO:

ANNOUNCER: Paul Temple is visited by Sir Graham Forbes of Scotland Yard and by a Mr Philip Kaufman who is attached to the Special Branch. Kaufman tells Paul Temple about a notorious criminal known as Dr Belasco. Temple promises to try and discover the identity of Belasco and during the course of certain investigations makes the acquaintance of the following suspects: Mrs Forester, Joseph – a servant of Mrs Forester, Henry Worth, Ed Bellamy, the proprietor of the Machicha Club – and a certain Mr David Nelson.

CUT TO: The TEMPLES' Lounge.

TEMPLE: Hello! What's this?

TEMPLE picks up a newspaper from the settee.

STEVE: It's the evening paper. They've got the Forester story on the front page.

TEMPLE: So I see. It's not a very good photograph of her, is it?

STEVE: I didn't think it was too bad. After all, newspaper photographs are never very good –

STEVE breaks off as the door is suddenly thrown open.

CHARLIE: I beg your pardon, m'm ...

STEVE: Charlie!

TEMPLE: What the devil – Why, Mr Nelson!

STEVE: What's the meaning of this, Mr Nelson?

NELSON: (*Perturbed and excited*) I'm sorry to crash in like this, Mrs Temple, it's quite unforgiveable I know, but – well ...

TEMPLE: That's all right, Charlie – you can go.

CHARLIE: Sir.

CHARLIE leaves, closing the door.

TEMPLE: Now – what is it?

NELSON: You've seen tonight's papers?

TEMPLE: Yes.

NELSON: About Mrs Forester, I mean – about her being dead?

TEMPLE: Of course.

NELSON: Well, that's just the point!

STEVE: What do you mean?

NELSON: She's not dead!

STEVE: Not dead?

NELSON: I saw her myself half an hour ago!

STEVE: I don't believe it!

TEMPLE: (*Calmly*) Where did you see her?

NELSON: (*Quickly: without thinking*) I saw her coming out of the house in Berkeley House Place. I … (*He hesitates*)

TEMPLE: Go on.

NELSON: (*Extremely on edge*) You don't believe me, do you?

TEMPLE: Well, I must confess I find it rather difficult to believe you.

STEVE: You must be mistaken, Mr Nelson!

NELSON: I'm not mistaken! I tell you I saw Mrs Forester as clearly as I can see you now.

TEMPLE: You say you saw her come out of the house in Berkeley House Place?

NELSON: Yes.

TEMPLE: When?

NELSON: I've told you: about half an hour ago.

TEMPLE: Were you watching the house?

NELSON: Well …

TEMPLE: Well, were you?

NELSON: Yes, I suppose I was.

TEMPLE: Why?

NELSON: I'll be frank with you. I've always believed that Mrs Forester was Dr Belasco. When I read that she had been killed in a motor accident, I just couldn't believe it. I had a strange sort of feeling that …

TEMPLE: That what?

NELSON: That it wasn't true. I don't know what made me think that. I went down to the house. I've been there before, you know that … I stood watching it. I must have been there, oh, about ten minutes or so when suddenly the door opened, and Mrs Forester came out. There was a car waiting for her.

TEMPLE: What was she dressed in?

NELSON: She had a fur coat on, the collar was turned up but –

TEMPLE: If the collar of the coat was turned up, how can you be so sure that it was Mrs Forester?

NELSON: Good heavens, I know her! I've seen her dozens of times.

TEMPLE: Go on.

NELSON: She got into the car and drove away.

TEMPLE: Did you take the number of the car?

NELSON: No, I'm afraid I didn't, I was … so surprised at seeing her that it never entered my head.

TEMPLE: Did this person you believe to be Mrs Forester –

NELSON: It <u>was</u> Mrs Forester!

TEMPLE: Well – did she see you?

NELSON: Oh, I don't know. I was sitting in my car on the other side of the road. Well, she must have noticed the car, but whether she actually noticed me or not, I … I wouldn't like to say.

STEVE: What sort of a coat was she wearing, Mr Nelson – what sort of fur, I mean?

NELSON: It was a mink coat. Dark mink, it had full sleeves and – my dear Mrs Temple, it was Mrs Forester all right!

TEMPLE: Have you told anyone else about this?

NELSON: No.

TEMPLE: You came straight here?

NELSON: No, I went back to my flat and had a drink. I was rather shaken.

TEMPLE: You felt as if you needed one?

NELSON: (*Laughs*) Yes! … Temple?

TEMPLE: Yes?

NELSON: I've got a hunch that you're not exactly surprised by all this.

TEMPLE: You're right, I'm not.

NELSON: I did see Mrs Forester, didn't I?

TEMPLE: Yes – I think you must have done.

STEVE: But, Paul! He couldn't!

TEMPLE: Steve, listen. For some months now, ever since he arrived in this country in fact, Dr Belasco has carefully thrown suspicion on Mrs Forester. Recently, a series of developments indicated beyond any shadow of doubt that Mrs Forester was Dr Belasco; accordingly, Sir Graham issued a warrant for her arrest. I knew this would happen, however, and I told Inspector Perry that under no circumstances must Mrs Forester be arrested. The motor car accident was faked.

STEVE: But, darling, you can't hope to get away with that.

TEMPLE: I don't hope to get away with it, Steve, not indefinitely. But for twenty-four hours, perhaps even forty-eight hours ... Yes. And a lot can happen in forty-eight hours, Steve.

NELSON: But why do you think Sir Graham is wrong – about Mrs Forester, I mean?

TEMPLE: Why do you think he's right?

NELSON: But surely, he must be right! Everything points to her being Dr Belasco.

TEMPLE: Not quite everything. One could, for instance, make out a pretty good case against Mr Worth.

NELSON: Worth? (*Faintly impressed*) Ah, yes, I suppose one could ...

TEMPLE: Or Joseph for that matter.

NELSON: Joseph?

TEMPLE: He works for Mrs Forester.

NELSON: I'd forgotten about Joseph ...

TEMPLE: And then, of course, there's yourself, Nelson.

NELSON: (*Starting to laugh*) Now, of course, you're just being ridiculous. (*He continues to laugh*)

TEMPLE: (*Quietly*) Let's all have a very large drink.

Play Incidental Music.

CUT TO: The TEMPLES' Dining Room.
It is breakfast time.

STEVE: Some more coffee, darling?

TEMPLE: M'm? Oh, thank you, Steve.

STEVE pours coffee.

STEVE: Paul ...

TEMPLE: Yes?

STEVE: I couldn't get to sleep last night for thinking about this Belasco affair. I kept turning over in my mind all the possible suspects.

179

TEMPLE: (*Lightly*) All the possible suspects? You must have kept yourself pretty busy!

STEVE: There are half-a-dozen of them.

TEMPLE: Half-a-dozen! Not that many, surely, Steve.

STEVE: Well, Mrs Forester – 1, Joseph – 2, Mr Bellamy – 3, Henry Worth – 4, David Nelson – 5, and Mr Kaufman – 6.

TEMPLE: Kaufman! You're not really serious about Kaufman? I keep telling you he's a man of great integrity.

STEVE: So was Inspector Dale – remember?

TEMPLE: (*A moment: seriously*) Yes, dear – I remember.

STEVE: Paul, I've been meaning to ask you. Have you discovered why the lighter Ross Morgan carried was identically the same as Mr Nelson's?

TEMPLE: Yes. Why, don't you see, Steve. Belasco forms an organisation – but the members of the organisation are not necessarily known to each other, so they have – in case of an emergency – a means of identification.

STEVE: They each carry identically the same kind of cigarette lighter!

TEMPLE: Exactly.

STEVE: Then Nelson's wife must have been a member of Belasco's organisation!

TEMPLE: Because Nelson got the cigarette lighter from her?

STEVE: Yes.

TEMPLE: How do you know that? We've only got his word for it. Steve, you heard Nelson last night – you heard what he said about visiting Mrs Forester's.

STEVE: Well?

TEMPLE: Well, didn't his story strike you as being rather inconsistent?

STEVE: What do you mean?

TEMPLE: In the first place he said that when he read that Mrs Forester had been killed in a car accident, he didn't believe it. He even went so far as to visit her house in fact. Suddenly, according to his story, his suspicions are confirmed, and Mrs Forester appears. What happens? Nelson – who apparently expected to see Mrs Forester – is so overcome by surprise that he immediately dashes back to his flat and mixes himself a whisky and soda.

STEVE: M'm. (*After a moment*) Paul, you know that man you found at Reiford – the man who drove the lorry?

TEMPLE: Abel Dunne? Yes.

STEVE: Well – do you think he was murdered?

TEMPLE: I'm pretty sure he was murdered.

STEVE: But you don't quite know how it was done?

TEMPLE: We know <u>how</u> it was done, darling – he was shot. But we don't know who did it.

STEVE: Did you examine the window, Paul, because –

TEMPLE: Yes, I examined the window, and Bellamy didn't shoot him through the window, if that's what you're thinking. He hadn't even reached the cottage when we heard the revolver shot.

STEVE: You know, Paul, I don't really understand this business about Mrs Forester. Does Sir Graham know that she's not dead?

TEMPLE: He does now. I telephoned Perry last night and told him to break the news to the old boy.

STEVE: But what's the point of it, darling?

TEMPLE:	I should have thought the point would have been perfectly obvious. If Belasco believes that –

The door opens.

TEMPLE:	What is it, Charlie?
CHARLIE:	I beg your pardon, sir, but Sir Graham Forbes is here, sir.
TEMPLE:	(*A moment's hesitation*) Ask him in, Charlie.
CHARLIE:	(*Going*) Yes, sir.
STEVE:	I'll bet he's absolutely furious with you.
TEMPLE:	I'll bet he is. (*Getting up*) Hello, Sir Graham. Come in! We're just having breakfast.
FORBES:	Good morning, Steve.
STEVE:	Would you like some coffee?
FORBES:	I should like some coffee very much.
TEMPLE:	What's the matter, Sir Graham? You don't appear to be your usual light-hearted self this morning!
FORBES:	I don't feel particularly light-hearted, Temple. Now what's all this nonsense about Mrs Forester? I sent Perry to Greenchurch with a warrant for her arrest, he returns with the information that she has been killed in a car accident, and I am now politely informed that she hasn't been killed at all –
TEMPLE:	(*Interrupting FORBES*) Sir Graham.
FORBES:	Well?

TEMPLE:	You remember when we were down at Greenchurch and Steve and I visited Camberley Lodge?
FORBES:	Yes.
TEMPLE:	Well – after Joseph and I discovered Braddock in the shrubbery at the back of the house I ... went back to the house and had rather an interesting conversation with Mrs Forester.
FORBES:	You never told me that, Temple!
TEMPLE:	No. As a matter of fact, I bullied her into telling me quite an interesting story.
FORBES:	What did she tell you?
TEMPLE:	Well, at first, she refused to tell me anything. I think she was a little embarrassed because Steve was there. (*Start FADE*) Suddenly, I realised this, and I told Steve to go back to the car and tell you exactly what had transpired ...

CUT TO: MRS FORESTER's Sitting Room at Camberley Lodge.

TEMPLE:	Go back to the car, Steve. Tell Sir Graham what's happened and ask him to get in touch with the local people. I'll stay here until you return.
STEVE:	Yes, all right, Paul.
TEMPLE:	Are you frightened of walking down the drive on your own?
STEVE:	Well ...
JOSEPH:	Where is your car, sir?

TEMPLE:	It's on the main road, Joseph, not far from the cottage you mentioned.
JOSEPH:	Well, if you wish to remain here, sir, until the police arrive, perhaps I could escort Mrs Temple back to the car?
STEVE:	No, there's no necessity, I shall be perfectly all right.
JOSEPH:	Very good, Madam.
STEVE:	(*Going*) Well, see you later, darling!
TEMPLE:	Yes, Steve,

The door opens and closes as STEVE leaves.

MRS FORESTER:	Now, if you'll excuse me, Mr Temple, I'm going to my room until the police arrive –
TEMPLE:	One moment, Mrs Forester, please.
MRS FORESTER:	(*Coldly*) Yes?
TEMPLE:	There are one or two questions I'd like to ask you.
MRS FORESTER:	I've answered all the questions I intend to answer until the police arrive, so if you'll kindly excuse me –
TEMPLE:	(*Very firmly*) Sit down.
MRS FORESTER:	I beg your pardon!
TEMPLE:	You heard what I said, sit down.
MRS FORESTER:	Mr Temple, I wish to go to my room, so if you'll kindly let me pass –
TEMPLE:	Sit down, Mrs Forester – before I get tough.
MRS FORESTER:	Joseph!
JOSEPH:	Mr Temple, I don't think you quite realise what you're saying, sir! This is Mrs Forester's house, she's quite at liberty to retire to her room if she wishes to do so.

TEMPLE:	Quite at liberty, Joseph – but not just at the moment! Now sit down, Mrs Forester, and listen to what I've got to say!
JOSEPH:	Mr Temple, I must ask you to –
MRS FORESTER:	That's all right, Joseph.

A moment.

TEMPLE:	Now you're being sensible.
JOSEPH:	Do you wish me to remain, Madam?
MRS FORESTER:	(*After a moment's hesitation*) No, you can go, Joseph.
JOSEPH:	(*Going*) Thank you, Madam.

The door opens and closes and JOSEPH leaves.

MRS FORESTER:	Now, what is it you want to ask me? If it's about that man – the man you've just found, I can … only say I have never seen him in my life before. I don't know who he is or where he's come from!
TEMPLE:	His name's Braddock. He was sent down here by Sir Graham Forbes. (*Watching MRS FORESTER*) However, let's forget Mr Braddock, shall we, and talk about a friend of yours.
MRS FORESTER:	A friend of mine?
TEMPLE:	Yes. Mr Worth.
MRS FORESTER:	Mr Worth!
TEMPLE:	Now don't tell me you've never heard of Mr Worth!
MRS FORESTER:	Yes, of course I have, but – well – you'd hardly call him a friend of mine.
TEMPLE:	He visited your house – in Town, I mean.

MRS FORESTER: (*A moment, then*) Yes, as a matter of fact, he did.

TEMPLE: (*Bluntly*) Why?

MRS FORESTER: I beg your pardon?

TEMPLE: I said: why did he visit your house?

MRS FORESTER: Because … Why are you asking these questions? Mr Worth's got nothing whatsoever to do with what happened.

TEMPLE: Mrs Forester!

MRS FORESTER: Yes?

TEMPLE: Don't let's beat about the bush! You know why I'm here, you know why I'm asking these questions. I'm investigating the Belasco affair, and I've every intention of getting the information I want.

MRS FORESTER: I've nothing to do with Belasco! I swear it!

TEMPLE: Mrs Forester, I've got a shrewd suspicion that Sir Graham Forbes is under the impression that you are Dr Belasco, therefore –

MRS FORESTER: What!

TEMPLE: – Therefore, when he learns about Braddock, it's ten to one –

MRS FORESTER: Mr Temple! You don't think that I'm Belasco!

TEMPLE: Why did Henry Worth visit your house, Mrs Forester? Why did you send a man like Harry Marx an invitation to your cocktail party? Why did you lie to me the night that you visited the Machicha?

MRS FORESTER: (*Softly*) What do you mean?

TEMPLE: You knew perfectly well that Joseph was at the Machicha – you went there to meet him, didn't you? Didn't you?

MRS FORESTER: (*A moment*) Yes.

TEMPLE: Why?

MRS FORESTER: Because …

MRS FORESTER hesitates; she is obviously under an emotional strain.

TEMPLE: Well?

MRS FORESTER: Because … About six years ago, just before my husband died, he became involved in a case known as the Hamish-Frinton Deal.

TEMPLE: (*Rather surprised*) I remember that case well – it was a new flotation that a man called Elliot Brook was trying.

MRS FORESTER: Elliot Brook was my husband – after he died, I reverted to my maiden name. Elliot was tried on an embezzlement charge and acquitted. Three months later he died.

TEMPLE: Go on.

MRS FORESTER: Elliot was guilty. However, certain important documents disappeared just before the trial started.

TEMPLE: Well?

MRS FORESTER: Those documents are still in existence. I've been trying to buy them.

TEMPLE: In order to destroy them?

MRS FORESTER: Yes.

TEMPLE: Did Worth claim to have possession of the documents?

MRS FORESTER: Worth said that he could find them for me. He put me in touch with a man called Harry Marx. Marx was – well – he was rather a peculiar type. To put it bluntly, he was something of a snob; he insisted on meeting my friends and being invited to all my cocktail parties. I was frightened to offend the little beast because I really felt that ultimately, he would get the papers.

TEMPLE: Go on.

MRS FORESTER: When Marx was murdered, I realised that my best plan was to get in touch with an associate of his – a man called Bellamy.

TEMPLE: Bellamy owns the Machicha – yes, I know Bellamy.

MRS FORESTER: I sent Joseph to the Machicha and he spoke to Bellamy. Bellamy was surprised – he didn't like Joseph and he insisted on meeting me before … committing himself. When I arrived at the Machicha, Joseph introduced me to Ed Bellamy, and he advised me to contact a man called Abel Dunne.

TEMPLE: Did you contact him?

MRS FORESTER: Joseph telephoned him on my behalf but …

TEMPLE: But I answered the telephone?

MRS FORESTER: Yes.

TEMPLE: Mrs Forester, about this rather incriminating document …

MRS FORESTER: Yes?

TEMPLE: It wouldn't concern you by any chance, as well as your husband?

MRS FORESTER: … That's beside the point, Mr Temple.

TEMPLE: As you say, Mrs Forester, that's beside
                     the point. Now tell me. How –
MRS FORESTER:How does Joseph fit into all of this? I
                     knew you'd ask that one sooner or
                     later.
TEMPLE: Well?
MRS FORESTER:Joseph used to work for my sister.
                     Before the war she had a villa on the
                     Riviera and Joseph – well – I suppose
                     you'd call him a ... very old friend of
                     the family.
TEMPLE: You trust him?
MRS FORESTER:Oh, explicitly! He's a very intelligent
                     person, you know, and a born
                     organiser. I leave all my personal
                     affairs to Joseph, and I can assure you
                     they are in very capable hands.
TEMPLE: ... I'm sure they are, Mrs Forester.
Start FADE of scene.
MRS FORESTER:Now, may I go to my room? Or have
                     you any further questions you wish to
                     ask me?
TEMPLE: No, you may go, Mrs Forester.
COMPLETE FADE.

CUT TO: The TEMPLES' Dining Room. As before.
TEMPLE: ... About a quarter of an hour later, you
                     returned with Steve and the
                     Greenchurch people.
FORBES: M'm. But you know, Temple, I still
                     don't understand your attitude over this
                     business. Supposing Mrs Forester was
                     telling the truth. Why did you take the
                     trouble to –

TEMPLE: (*Interrupting FORBES*) Sir Graham, for several weeks now, Belasco has been throwing suspicion on to Mrs Forester, so I decided to find out what exactly would happen once Belasco was under the impression that Mrs Forester was dead.

STEVE: It's obvious what'll happen, he'll shift the suspicion on to someone else.

FORBES: Well, supposing Steve is right, and he does shift the suspicion on to someone else – where does that get us?

TEMPLE: (*Lightly*) It gets us down to a question of simple arithmetic, doesn't it? Two from six leaves four and ...

FORBES: You mean we can forget Mrs Forester, and concentrate ...

TEMPLE: Exactly!

FORBES: Yes, but ... Tell me, does anyone else know about Mrs Forester?

TEMPLE: You know, Perry knows –

FORBES: And Kaufman.

TEMPLE: (*Casually*) You told Kaufman?

FORBES: Yes, he was with me last night when Perry telephoned.

STEVE: And don't forget Mr Nelson, darling.

FORBES: (*Surprised*) Nelson?

TEMPLE: Nelson was watching the house last night and saw Mrs Forester leave. I feel annoyed about that because I told Perry to take particular care ...

TEMPLE is interrupted by the ringing of the telephone.

STEVE: It's all right, Paul, I'll take it.

STEVE lifts the receiver.

STEVE: (*On the phone*) Hello? Who is that?

KAUFMAN: (*On the other end*) Hello? Who is that?

STEVE: Mr Kaufman?

KAUFMAN: Yes.

STEVE: This is Mrs Temple.

KAUFMAN: Oh! I am so sorry, Mrs Temple, I did not recognise you! Is Sir Graham with you at the moment?

STEVE: Yes, would you like a word with him?

KAUFMAN: If you please.

STEVE: (*Aside to FORBES*) It's Mr Kaufman, Sir Graham.

FORBES: Oh!

FORBES takes the receiver.

FORBES: Thank you. (*On the phone*) Kaufman?

KAUFMAN: I'm afraid I've got some bad news for you, Sir Graham. The National Fur Warehouse was broken into just after four o'clock this morning.

FORBES: Belasco?

KAUFMAN: Well, quite obviously Belasco was behind it, sir.

FORBES: How much did they get away with?

KAUFMAN: Fortunately, they were disturbed – I should say about £15,000 worth. But there's rather an interesting point, Sir Graham …

FORBES: Well?

KAUFMAN: Inspector Perry found a pencil – a small silver pencil. It was found near the side gate where they apparently forced an entrance. He swears it belongs to Mr Bellamy.

FORBES: Mr Bellamy.

KAUFMAN: Yes.

FORBES: M'm. Well, thank you, Kaufman. I shall be at the office in about an hour.

KAUFMAN: Very good, sir.

FORBES replaces the receiver.

TEMPLE: Well?

FORBES: Apparently, Dr Belasco has switched suspicion on to Mr Bellamy ...

Play Incidental Music.

CUT TO: The Machicha Club.

The dance orchestra is playing.

PERRY: Good evening, Mr Temple – I'm sorry we're a little on the late side.

TEMPLE: That's all right, Inspector, as a matter of fact, I've only just arrived myself.

KAUFMAN: (*Arriving*) Good evening!

TEMPLE: Oh, good evening, Kaufman.

KAUFMAN: Have you seen Bellamy?

TEMPLE: Not yet.

PERRY: Don't worry, he knows we're here all right! If the truth was known, I expect he's watching us at this very moment.

TEMPLE: I wouldn't be surprised.

KAUFMAN: Have you got the pencil with you?

PERRY: Aye.

KAUFMAN: You're sure it is Bellamy's?

PERRY: Quite sure.

KAUFMAN: All right, let's see what he's got to say about it.

TEMPLE: Kaufman –

KAUFMAN: Yes?

TEMPLE: Don't you think it might be rather a good idea if one of us stayed down here? I

	mean, supposing Bellamy gets tough and decides to make a dash for it?
KAUFMAN:	Yes, perhaps you're right. I'll wait in the hall near the main entrance – near the telephone box.
PERRY:	Right. Come along, Mr Temple.

CUT TO: BELLAMY's Office.

A knock at the door.

BELLAMY:	(*Pleasantly*) Come in!

The door opens and TEMPLE and PERRY enter.

BELLAMY:	Come in, Inspector! Hello, Mr Temple!
TEMPLE:	Bellamy.
BELLAMY:	Where's the other guy? Don't tell me he baled out!

BELLAMY closes the door.

PERRY:	I suppose you've been watching us through that perishing periscope of yours.
BELLAMY:	Sure! Well – sit down! Sit down! Now what can I get you – a scotch and soda?
PERRY:	Not for me.
BELLAMY:	Mr Temple?

TEMPLE shakes his head.

BELLAMY:	No? O.K. – we'll skip it.
PERRY:	Bellamy – you remember that silver pencil of yours? Eh, the small one with the –
BELLAMY:	Sure! Sure, I remember it!
PERRY:	Have you still got it?
BELLAMY:	Why, yes!
PERRY:	Where is it?
BELLAMY:	Why, it's in this drawer!

BELLAMY opens a drawer.

BELLAMY:	That's funny …
TEMPLE:	Can't you find it?

BELLAMY: Well – it must be here somewhere!

BELLAMY turns over papers, etc.

TEMPLE: When did you see it last?

BELLAMY: Why, only the other – Say, what's all this about anyway?

PERRY produces the pencil.

PERRY: Is this your pencil, Mr Bellamy?

BELLAMY: Why, yes! You know darn tooting well that's my – Say, where did you get that?

PERRY: I found it – or rather Sergeant Lester did.

BELLAMY: Where?

PERRY: He found it this morning near one of the side entrances to the National Fur Warehouse …

BELLAMY: The National Fur … That place was knocked off last night, it's in the papers, why – What is this – a check-up?

PERRY: You can call it that, if you like.

BELLAMY: What else is it? … O.K. go on, let's have it!

PERRY: Where were you last night?

BELLAMY: I was here, at the club – I arrived about a quarter past eight.

PERRY: What time did you leave?

BELLAMY: Just after five.

TEMPLE: This morning?

BELLAMY: Yeah.

TEMPLE: Wasn't that rather late?

BELLAMY: Sure.

TEMPLE: What time do you usually leave?

BELLAMY: Oh, it varies – usually between half-past one or two.

TEMPLE: What made you so late this morning?

BELLAMY:	My accountant dropped in; we had to do a certain amount of work on the books.
TEMPLE:	Who is your accountant?
BELLAMY:	A man called Demming – Charlie Demming.
PERRY:	Demming, Seaman and Brooks?
BELLAMY:	Yes.
TEMPLE:	(*To PERRY*) Do you know them?
PERRY:	Aye, they're very reliable people.
TEMPLE:	What time did Mr Demming arrive?
BELLAMY:	About ten o'clock.
TEMPLE:	And he left?
BELLAMY:	He left with me – just after five.
TEMPLE:	Did anyone see you leave?
BELLAMY:	No, I don't think – Oh, yeah! Sergeant Carter. He was passing the door just as we were going out!
PERRY:	Did he see you?
BELLAMY:	Of course, he did! As a matter of fact, we had a chat. I introduced him to Mr Demming. Gee, I guess I've been kind of lucky! I mean, if I'd gone home last night at the usual time and gone straight to bed, I ... Boy, I've certainly been lucky!
PERRY:	(*Quietly*) You certainly have, Mr Bellamy.

Play Incidental Music.

CUT TO: The TEMPLES' Bedroom.

TEMPLE is whistling to himself; he is preparing for bed. Casually he takes out his watch, wallet, coppers, etc., and puts them down on the dressing table. STEVE is already in bed.

STEVE:	I suppose there's no doubt about Mr Bellamy's alibi?

TEMPLE: None whatsoever, he was telling the truth all right. It's been checked and double-checked. I don't want to be late tomorrow morning, darling!

STEVE: (*Tired*) I know what that means! You'll be snoring like a pig long after eight o'clock!

TEMPLE: For your information, I do not snore like a pig! I may purr occasionally –

STEVE: (*Yawning*) Gosh, I'm tired.

TEMPLE: Yes, well, move up, darling. I don't expect to have any bedclothes, but I would at least like to sleep on the mattress.

TEMPLE gets into bed.

STEVE: (*So sleepy you can hardly understand what she says*) What time is it?

TEMPLE: It's a quarter past eleven.

STEVE: I thought it was later than that.

TEMPLE: (*Yawning*) No, I don't think so.

STEVE: Paul …

TEMPLE: M'm?

STEVE: You know, I still think I'm right about Kaufman.

TEMPLE: You're always right, darling!

STEVE: Yes, well, I'm very sleepy. Goodnight …

TEMPLE: Goodnight …

We hear the bedroom clock ticking. Slowly, very slowly, TEMPLE commences to snore. The snoring develops and almost reaches a crescendo as the bedside telephone starts to ring.

TEMPLE: (*With a start*) What's that?

STEVE: It's you, darling – you've been making the most extraordinary noises.

TEMPLE: Me?

STEVE: (*Sleepily*) Yes …

196

TEMPLE: Surely, I don't make a noise like a bell!

STEVE: I wouldn't put it past you.

TEMPLE: It's the telephone …

TEMPLE lifts the receiver.

TEMPLE: (*On the phone*) Hello? Hello?

WORTH: (*On the other end: softly*) Mr Temple?

TEMPLE: Yes. Who is that?

WORTH: (*Rather nervously*) Mr Temple … listen … to the clock …

TEMPLE: What?

WORTH: Did you hear what I said? Listen to the clock.

TEMPLE: Who is that? Who –

WORTH has hung up. TEMPLE bangs the phone cradle up and down.

TEMPLE: What the devil …

STEVE: Paul, what is it?

TEMPLE: Well –

TEMPLE replaces the receiver.

TEMPLE: – it sounded to me like Worth, although I suppose it could have been Kaufman.

STEVE: What did he say?

TEMPLE: He said – Listen to the clock.

STEVE: Is that all he said?

TEMPLE: Yes.

STEVE: Well, what does he mean "listen to the clock"? Does he mean our clock? That clock on the mantlepiece?

TEMPLE: I suppose he must do …

We hear the clock ticking.

STEVE: I don't get it.

TEMPLE: I wonder if he … (*Suddenly*) What time is it? What time does the clock say?

STEVE: Why, it's a quarter past eleven.

TEMPLE: A quarter past eleven! But it was a quarter past eleven when we came to bed!

STEVE: All right, darling, there's no need to get excited, it only means that the clock's stopped and – (*She stops speaking*) – but it can't have stopped, we can hear it, we can …

TEMPLE and STEVE listen to the ticking noise.

STEVE: Paul, the hands aren't moving … the clock's ticking but … It must be …

TEMPLE: Stay where you are!

STEVE: What are you going to do?!

TEMPLE: Don't move!

TEMPLE crosses the room.

STEVE: Paul, darling …

TEMPLE picks up the clock.

TEMPLE: I've got it … I've got it …

TEMPLE starts to move towards the window and throws the clock through it. There is a tremendous smashing of glass followed by an explosion. STEVE utters a shriek.

STEVE: Oh, Paul, Paul …

The telephone starts to ring.

STEVE: Who's that? Paul, who is it?

A moment, then TEMPLE lifts the receiver.

TEMPLE: (*On the phone*) Hello?

On the other end of the line, JOSEPH sounds desperately ill and frightened.

JOSEPH: Mr Temple?

TEMPLE: Yes?

JOSEPH: This is Joseph, I … I …

TEMPLE: What is it, Joseph?

JOSEPH: I've got to see you, Mr Temple, it's … it's urgent, it's desperately urgent. I've … I've …

TEMPLE: Joseph, what is it? What's the matter?

JOSEPH: I've … I've got to see you. I've got to tell you about Belasco …

TEMPLE: Where are you? Where are you speaking from?

JOSEPH: I'm in a telephone box on the corner of Westley Street. I'm all shot to pieces, Mr Temple, they've … they've beaten me up … they've …

TEMPLE: Stay where you are, Joseph, I'll be there in five minutes!

TEMPLE bangs down the receiver.

STEVE: Paul, what is it? What's happened?

TEMPLE: Get dressed, darling! Be quick – get dressed!

The bedroom door is thrown open and CHARLIE rushes in.

CHARLIE:What's happened? I heard a blinking explosion like one of the old doodle-bugs!

TEMPLE picks up his car keys.

TEMPLE: Get the car out of the garage for me, Charlie. Here's the key. Catch – (*He throws the keys, Charlie catches them*) – Be quick!

CHARLIE:Okedoke!

Play Incidental Music.

CUT TO: The TEMPLES' Car.

The car is travelling very fast – then it slows down and comes to a standstill.

STEVE: There's the telephone box on the corner.

TEMPLE: You stay in the car, Steve.

STEVE: No, Paul, hadn't I better –

TEMPLE: Stay in the car, darling, please!

TEMPLE opens the car door.

TEMPLE: I shan't be a minute.

TEMPLE slams the car door.

CUT TO: Inside the Phone Box.

JOSEPH is obviously in great despair, breathing heavily and in pain. TEMPLE opens the door of the box.

JOSEPH: Who is it? Who is –

TEMPLE: It's me, Joseph – Temple. Are you badly hurt?

JOSEPH: It's … it's my back … my back and my face … they, they beat me … they beat me until … I couldn't stand it any longer. I couldn't stand it! I … I …

TEMPLE: Give me your arm, I'll get you over to the car.

JOSEPH: No! No! No, Mr Temple, you shouldn't have come here, you shouldn't have come!

TEMPLE: What do you mean? Why, you telephoned me. You –

JOSEPH: Don't you see? Don't you see? They … they made me telephone you, they … they made me do it, they made me … They beat me until I … (*Almost crying*) I had to do it or … or …

TEMPLE: (*Shaking JOSEPH*) What do you mean? Joseph, what do you mean!

A moment.

JOSEPH: (*Softly; weakly*) It's … it's a trap …

Closing Music.

END OF EPISODE SEVEN

EPISODE EIGHT

THE FINAL CURTAIN

OPEN TO:

ANNOUNCER: Paul Temple is visited by Sir Graham Forbes of Scotland Yard and by a Mr Philip Kaufman who is attached to the Special Branch. Kaufman tells Paul Temple about a notorious criminal known as Dr Belasco. Temple promises to try and discover the identity of Belasco and during the course of certain investigations makes the acquaintance of the following suspects: Mrs Forester, Joseph – a servant of Mrs Forester, Henry Worth, Ed Bellamy, the proprietor of the Machicha Club – and a certain Mr David Nelson. Late one night, Temple receives an urgent telephone call from Joseph. (*Start FADE*) Accompanied by Steve, Temple makes his way to the telephone box on the corner of Westley Street and Shaftesbury Avenue …

CUT TO: Inside the Phone Box.

JOSEPH is obviously in great despair, breathing heavily and in pain. TEMPLE opens the door of the box.

JOSEPH: No, Mr Temple, you shouldn't have come here, you shouldn't have come!

TEMPLE: What do you mean? Why, you telephoned me. You –

JOSEPH: Don't you see? Don't you see? They … they made me telephone you, they … they made me do it, they made me … They beat me until I … (*Almost crying*) I had to do it or … or …

TEMPLE: (*Shaking JOSEPH*) What do you mean? Joseph, what do you mean!

A moment.

JOSEPH: (*Softly; weakly*) It's … it's a trap …

TEMPLE: A trap!

JOSEPH: Yes … get back to the car and get away from here, or you'll … (*He faints*)

We hear the sound of footsteps as STEVE arrives.

STEVE: Paul, what's the matter with him?

TEMPLE: He's been beaten up, Steve.

STEVE: Oh, how horrible. (*A moment*) Is he dead?

TEMPLE: No. No, I don't think so – he's fainted. Steve – listen – They made Joseph telephone us – we've walked into a trap.

STEVE: A trap? But how on earth could we – (*She breaks off*) Look, there's a car coming.

The distant sound of an approaching car is heard.

TEMPLE: I wish I'd remembered that revolver in the dressing table, I could have –

STEVE: I did.

TEMPLE: Oh, good girl, Steve! Now get behind the telephone box! Quickly! Quickly!

TEMPLE and STEVE rush behind the telephone booth as the approaching car gathers speed.

STEVE: Who is it?

As the car passes the box, a revolver shot rings out, then a second shot, which smashes a glass pane in the side of the phone box.

TEMPLE: I think he's hit Joseph!

STEVE: Who's driving the car?

A third revolver shot from the car.

TEMPLE: Steve, keep behind the box! Now where's that revolver? Quickly, darling – where is it?

STEVE: Here we are …

TEMPLE: Good! Now keep behind the box!

STEVE: Oh, look out, Paul! Don't show yourself in case he –

TEMPLE: (*Taking aim*) I'm going to hit his blasted tyre if it's the last thing I do …!

TEMPLE fires. The shot rings out and is followed by the explosion of a burst tyre.

STEVE: You've hit it!

TEMPLE: By Timothy, I have!

The car commences to skid.

STEVE: He's skidding … He's skidding …

TEMPLE: Great Scot, he's turning over!

As TEMPLE speaks the car turns completely over: followed by the explosion of the petrol tank.

STEVE: Oh, Paul, look! Look! The car's on fire!

TEMPLE: Steve, go to Joseph – I'll see you in a minute!

STEVE: Yes, all right, but do be careful … Paul! There's someone climbing out of the car … Why – it's David Nelson!

CUT TO: Further down the Street.

TEMPLE runs up to the burning car.

TEMPLE: Nelson – don't move! Do you hear me, Nelson – don't move!

NELSON: (*Coughing*) Who is it? I can't see … it's this smoke, I … Ah, it's you, Temple!

TEMPLE: Don't move, Nelson! If you do, I warn you, I shall fire.

NELSON: You think you're damn clever –

TEMPLE: Keep your hand away from that pocket. Nelson, I warn you!

A moment.

NELSON: What do you want me to do?

TEMPLE: You know where the telephone box is – turn round – and walk towards it.

NELSON: And if I refuse?

TEMPLE: I shall pull this trigger.

A pause.

NELSON: Temple …

TEMPLE: Yes?

NELSON: Do you think I'm Dr Belasco?

A pause.

TEMPLE: Since you ask me, I think –

NELSON suddenly springs at TEMPLE.

TEMPLE: – Why, you …!

TEMPLE and NELSON struggle. The struggle develops. They are both fighting for the revolver.

NELSON: Give me that revolver … You give me that …

The fight continues. TEMPLE starts to become overpowered. STEVE runs up. There is a dull, heavy thud as STEVE hits NELSON, and with a gasp of surprise he falls.

STEVE: Paul, are you all right?

TEMPLE: Yes … Yes, I … Phew! … What did you hit him with?

STEVE: I found this spanner, as a matter of fact I nearly tripped over it.

TEMPLE: What about Joseph?

STEVE: He's dead, one of the bullets caught him on the side of the head and …

TEMPLE: Stay here with Nelson; I'm going across to the phone box.

STEVE: Paul …

TEMPLE: Yes, darling?

STEVE: Is David Nelson Dr Belasco?

A moment.

TEMPLE: No, Steve.

206

Play Incidental Music.

CUT TO: The TEMPLES' Bedroom.
The door opens, TEMPLE enters with a tray.

STEVE: (*Waking up*) What time is it?

TEMPLE: It's half-past eleven, Steve. I've brought you some coffee.

STEVE: Half-past eleven! Good heavens, I should have – Paul, you're dressed!

TEMPLE: Yes, I've been up for hours! I've been down to the Yard, darling, to see Sir Graham.

STEVE: (*Puzzled*) Paul …

TEMPLE: Here's your coffee.

STEVE: What are you laughing at?

TEMPLE: You look exactly like the morning after the night before.

STEVE: I feel exactly like the morning after the night before!

TEMPLE: Drink up your coffee, Steve.

STEVE drinks.

STEVE: Paul. If David Nelson isn't Dr Belasco, then how exactly does he fit into all this?

TEMPLE: Well, as you know, when Dr Belasco arrived in this country, he formed an organisation. Nelson was a member until he fell out with Belasco and –

STEVE: Started an organisation of his own?

TEMPLE: Exactly. He knew that his wife Rene was friendly with Mrs Forester, and he tried to persuade Rene to get certain information about Mrs Forester so that he could blackmail her. He was very anxious to lay his hands on the Hamish-Frinton

207

	document. This was the document that Mrs Forester's husband Elliot Brook –
STEVE:	Yes, I remember, darling. But why did Rene Nelson commit suicide?
TEMPLE:	Because she found out that her husband was mixed up with Belasco.
STEVE:	Then his story about her borrowing money from Mrs Forester was simply –
TEMPLE:	An attempt on Nelson's part to convince you that he was the kind, devoted husband endeavouring to solve the mystery of his wife's suicide.
STEVE:	Yes.
TEMPLE:	He added strength to the story by telling me that he had engaged a private enquiry agent.
STEVE:	But he did engage her, we saw her at the café.
TEMPLE:	Ah, Mary Hamilton was a member of the Nelson set up. She was planted at Worth's café by Nelson in order to watch Worth. Suddenly Nelson became suspicious – and found that she was playing in with Worth.
STEVE:	So he murdered her the night we arrived at the café.
TEMPLE:	Yes.
STEVE:	But how do you account for the fact that you found Nelson's cigarette lighter at Abel Dunne's flat?
TEMPLE:	Well, Belasco placed the lighter on the stairs in order to throw suspicion onto Nelson.
STEVE:	But …

TEMPLE:	But what?
STEVE:	Well, from what you say, I gather I was wrong about Kaufman, and Henry Worth is Belasco. But why should he warn us about that bomb last night in the clock?
TEMPLE:	As you say, if he's Dr Belasco, why should he do that?
STEVE:	Yes … Paul, what about Joseph?
TEMPLE:	Nelson tried to force Joseph to go in with him, as Joseph knew a great deal about Mrs Forester and her friends and would have been a valuable asset to Nelson. But Joseph refused and was beaten up. Then suddenly Nelson hit upon the idea of getting Joseph to telephone me, and –

TEMPLE is interrupted by a knock on the door.

STEVE:	Yes, come in.

The door opens.

CHARLIE:	I beg your pardon, Ma'am.
TEMPLE:	What is it, Charlie?
CHARLIE:	Inspector Perry's here, sir, with Mr Kaufman – they'd like a word with you.
TEMPLE:	Inspector Perry?
CHARLIE:	Yes, sir.
TEMPLE:	(*After a tiny pause*) Yes, all right, Charlie. Tell them I shan't be a moment.
CHARLIE:	O.K.

CHARLIE leaves, closing the door.

TEMPLE:	Now, I wonder what Inspector Perry wants, it's rather odd that he – …

TEMPLE stops a moment.

STEVE:	Did you see Perry – at the Yard, I mean?

TEMPLE: ... No, I only saw Sir Graham ... (*A sudden decision*) I'll be back in a minute, darling.

CUT TO: The TEMPLES' Lounge.

KAUFMAN: ... I quite agree with what you say, my dear Inspector, but if, on the other hand, Worth deliberately telephoned Temple with the intention –

KAUFMAN breaks off as the door opens and TEMPLE enters.

TEMPLE: Good morning, Gentlemen!

KAUFMAN: (*Amiably*) Ah, so here you are, Monsieur!

PERRY: Good morning, Mr Temple.

TEMPLE: Good morning, Inspector – what can I do for you?

PERRY: Sir Graham asked me to tell you that the meeting's been called for three o'clock, sir – it's in Superintendent Bradley's office.

TEMPLE: Three o'clock – yes, all right, Inspector, I'll be there.

PERRY: (*Hesitating: then significantly*) We're, eh ... picking up Mr Worth this morning, sir.

TEMPLE: You're what – you mean a warrant?

PERRY: Yes, sir.

TEMPLE: (*Not too pleased*) Whose idea is that? Mr Kaufman's?

KAUFMAN: (*Calmy*) Have you any objection?

TEMPLE: You think that Worth –

KAUFMAN: (*A sudden note of authority*) I think that we are drawing very near to the final curtain, Mr Temple. Worth is implicated in this business so we cannot afford to take any risks.

210

TEMPLE: Does that mean that you think …

KAUFMAN: … That I think Worth is Dr Belasco?

TEMPLE: Yes.

KAUFMAN: It means precisely what I say. (*Watching TEMPLE*) We cannot afford to take any risks.

A slight pause.

TEMPLE: (*Quite pleasantly*) Well … can I get you a drink?

KAUFMAN: (*Briskly*) No. No, thank you. We must be going.

PERRY: Three o'clock, Mr Temple.

TEMPLE: Yes, three o'clock, Inspector – thank you.

Start to FADE SCENE.

KAUFMAN: And how is Mrs Temple this morning? I trust that your unfortunate experience last night has not unduly perturbed …

CUT TO: The TEMPLES' Bedroom.

The door opens and TEMPLE enters, moving briskly to the telephone.

TEMPLE: Hello! Have you gone to sleep again, Steve?!

TEMPLE lifts the receiver and starts to dial.

STEVE: (*Yawning*) Good gracious, I … Darling, I don't think I shall ever get up today! (*TEMPLE laughs*) What did Mr Kaufman want?

TEMPLE: Oh, nothing very much – there's a meeting called for three o'clock.

STEVE: Who are you telephoning?

TEMPLE: Worth.

We can hear the number ringing out.

211

STEVE: Worth? But why are you telephoning Worth?

TEMPLE: You'll hear … (*On the phone*) Hello?

WORTH: (*On the other end*) Hello?

TEMPLE: Mr Worth?

WORTH: (*Nervously*) Who is that?

TEMPLE: This is Temple here …

WORTH: (*Still nervous, but relieved*) Oh, hello, Mr Temple. How are you this morning?

TEMPLE: Alive and kicking – thanks to you, my friend.

WORTH: You found it all right?

TEMPLE: Yes, I found it all right – otherwise I shouldn't be talking to you.

WORTH: I didn't know what to do, Mr Temple – I was desperately worried, and I just didn't know what to do.

TEMPLE: How did you know about it?

WORTH: I overheard Belasco giving instructions to one of his men – it was quite by accident. But I realised what was going on and decided to telephone you.

TEMPLE: Well, one good turn deserves another, Mr Worth.

WORTH: (*A little frightened*) What do you mean?

TEMPLE: You've got about fifteen minutes – they've got a warrant out for you. Perry's on his way to the café.

WORTH: A warrant for me?

TEMPLE: Yes.

WORTH: Is this the truth, Mr Temple?

TEMPLE: Yes. Worth, tell me: that night you turned up at Abel Dunne's.

WORTH: Well?

TEMPLE: Did Belasco send you there?

WORTH: But of course. I told you the truth that night, Mr Temple, I swear I did, I … But you must realise I told you the truth, you must realise it, because …

TEMPLE: Because what?

WORTH: Because you know the identity of Dr Belasco – don't you?

TEMPLE: Yes.

WORTH: Mr Temple, you're not joking about the warrant?

TEMPLE: No, I'm not joking.

WORTH: Well – thanks for the tip.

TEMPLE: Goodbye, Worth – and good luck.

WORTH: Auf-wiedersehn.

STEVE: Paul!

TEMPLE: (*His thoughts elsewhere*) Yes?

TEMPLE replaces the receiver.

STEVE: Then Henry Worth isn't Dr Belasco?!

TEMPLE: No, darling. Henry Worth isn't Dr Belasco.

Play Incidental Music.

CUT TO: The TEMPLE's Lounge.

FADE UP on TEMPLE mixing drinks, then passing one to SIR GRAHAM.

TEMPLE: Here we are, Sir Graham.

FORBES: Thank you.

TEMPLE: Skoal!

FORBES: Skoal!

TEMPLE and SIR GRAHAM drink.

TEMPLE: What's on your mind?

FORBES: I'm rather worried, Temple. I feel somehow that …

TEMPLE: That what?

213

FORBES: Well, to be frank, I'm not so sure that Steve should be in on this. You know Belasco, you know exactly –

TEMPLE: I agree, Sir Graham – but you try and keep Steve out of it. I'm darned if I can. Once a newspaper woman, always a newspaper woman. (*Casually*) By the way, did Perry pick up Worth this morning?

FORBES: No, he didn't – I've got a shrewd suspicion someone tipped him off.

TEMPLE: Tipped him off! Really! That's extraordinary!

FORBES: (*Drily*) Most extraordinary.

TEMPLE: Will you have another drink?

FORBES: No, thank you.

TEMPLE: This man, Sir Graham, the man that's tailing Belasco – he's completely reliable, I take it?

FORBES: Completely reliable. Temple, you're sure – quite sure, aren't you, that –

TEMPLE: Quite sure, Sir Graham.

FORBES: It seems extraordinary!

The telephone starts to ring.

FORBES: I'd have bet my bottom dollar that it was –

TEMPLE: Excuse me.

TEMPLE lifts the receiver.

TEMPLE: (*On the phone*) Hello?

GIRL: (*On the other end*) Mr Temple?

TEMPLE: Yes?

GIRL: This is the Machicha Club – hold the line, please, Mr Bellamy wants you.

BELLAMY: (*Coming on the line*) Hello, there! Mr Temple?

TEMPLE: Yes.

BELLAMY: Ed Bellamy here.

214

TEMPLE:	Hello, Bellamy, how are you?
BELLAMY:	I'm fine. What's going on around here?
TEMPLE:	What do you mean?
BELLAMY:	This place of mine is swarming with 'dicks'. It's lousy with 'em! (*TEMPLE laughs*) No but give us a break. I'm supposed to be running a night club – not a policeman's picnic!
TEMPLE:	That's all right, Bellamy – don't worry – it's positively for one performance only!
BELLAMY:	Yeah, but seriously, it's getting in my hair! There's only one well-dressed guy out of the whole bunch.
TEMPLE:	(*Laughing*) Don't tell me, that's Mr Kaufman?
BELLAMY:	Look, what's it all in aid of anyway?
TEMPLE:	You probably don't know it, Bellamy, but you've got a distinguished guest at the Machicha.
BELLAMY:	Not too distinguished I hope, or we shall be landed with the bill. Who is it anyway?
TEMPLE:	Dr Belasco.
BELLAMY:	(*Stunned*) Dr … are you kiddin'?
TEMPLE:	I'm not kidding anyone, Bellamy.
BELLAMY:	Dr Belasco! Is this on the level?
TEMPLE:	On the level.
BELLAMY:	Temple, are you … coming here tonight?
TEMPLE:	Yes, I shall be there with you in about half-an-hour. Incidentally, I shall probably want to use your office and borrow that periscope gadget of yours.
BELLAMY:	Yeah, that's O.K. I'll be on the lookout for you. You know where the office is.
TEMPLE:	I do. Goodbye!

BELLAMY: Goodbye.

TEMPLE replaces the receiver.

TEMPLE: That was Bellamy; he doesn't appear to be impressed by your colleagues, Sir Graham.

FORBES: (*Laconically*) He will be – when things get tough.

TEMPLE chuckles. The door opens and STEVE enters. She is obviously in high spirits, gay and determined.

STEVE: Hello, Sir Graham! How are you?

FORBES: I'm ... fine, thank you, Steve.

STEVE: Well, you don't look it – and you don't sound it either! You look very depressed! (*Swinging around*) Darling, do you like the dress?

TEMPLE moves to the drinks table.

TEMPLE: Yes, rather. But haven't I seen it before somewhere?

STEVE: Of course! It's the one you saw in South Audley Street – the one you said was too expensive.

TEMPLE: Oh, yes I thought – (*Dawning on him*) Oh, yes.

STEVE laughs.

FORBES: Steve ...

STEVE: Yes, Sir Graham?

FORBES: I do hope you won't think I'm being difficult if I ...

STEVE: ... If you suggest that I stay at home this evening?

FORBES: Yes.

STEVE: Paul, have you been getting on to Sir Graham, because –

216

TEMPLE:	I never said a word, darling. Honestly, I didn't! (*Approaching with a drink for STEVE*) In any case, I know what it is once you've made up your mind. Here's a cocktail.
STEVE:	Thanks.
FORBES:	I don't want to be difficult about this, Steve, but I do feel that –
STEVE:	Then don't be difficult, Sir Graham! (*On the move*) Good gracious, who on earth arranged those flowers – Charlie!
TEMPLE:	Steve, I do wish you would listen to Sir Graham.
FORBES:	You know perfectly well why we're going to the Machicha Club, Steve. We're picking up Belasco – and he may get awkward.
STEVE:	Sir Graham, I was in on the Belasco affair at the beginning and I have every intention of being in on it at the end! Nothing in the whole wide world would stop me from going to the Machicha Club tonight; so be a darling and don't waste your breath. Now mix me another drink, Paul – and then we'll be off.
TEMPLE:	(*Moving to the drinks table*) Good heavens, have you knocked that back already! Sir Graham?
FORBES:	Not for me, Temple.

TEMPLE mixes the drink and brings it to Steve.

TEMPLE:	Here we are, Steve.
STEVE:	Thank you.

FORBES: Steve, look here, supposing we compromised, and instead of you actually coming to the Machicha with us, you – (*He stops and stares at STEVE*) Is anything the matter?

STEVE: I don't know, I … Paul, I feel rather odd, I …

FORBES: What is it, Steve?

TEMPLE: What's the matter with you, darling?

STEVE: I … I don't know … I feel dizzy … I feel … Paul, I …

STEVE drops her drink. The glass smashes. STEVE faints, TEMPLE catches her.

FORBES: She's fainted!

TEMPLE: It's all right – I've got her.

FORBES: Lay her down on the settee.

TEMPLE puts STEVE on the settee.

FORBES: Temple, what is it?

TEMPLE: It's all right, Sir Graham. I gave her a sleeping draught. She's spark out – she'll be out for hours.

FORBES: (*Laughing*) Temple, you are the limit.

TEMPLE: Nothing, nothing in the whole wide world would stop me from going to the Machicha Club tonight! Good old Steve! Come along, Sir Graham! Don't worry about Steve, she'll be all right!

Play Incidental Music.

CUT TO: The Machicha Club Foyer.

At the cloakroom. The dance orchestra plays in the distance.

ATTENDANT: I'll put both your coats together, sir.

FORBES: Thank you.

218

TEMPLE:	I'll take the ticket.
ATTENDANT:	Very good, sir. (*Accepting a tip*) Oh, thank you, sir.
PERRY:	(*Business-like*) Good evening, sir.
FORBES:	Evening, Perry.
PERRY:	Good evening, Mr Temple.
TEMPLE:	Evening, Inspector.
FORBES:	Everything all right, Perry?
PERRY:	Yes, sir – nothing to report, sir. He's still here, sir.
FORBES:	Good. Come along, Temple.

CUT TO: The Club Restaurant.

The orchestra is playing, people are dining and dancing.

WAITER:	Good evening, gentlemen.
TEMPLE:	Good evening. I believe you have a table reserved for me – Mr Temple.
WAITER:	But of course – this way please, sir.
TEMPLE:	Thank you.

The WAITER leads TEMPLE and FORBES across the dance floor.

FORBES:	(*Aside*) There's Kaufman.
TEMPLE:	Yes.

They arrive at the table.

WAITER:	Here we are, sir – your waiter will be along in a moment.
FORBES:	Thank you.

The orchestra stops. There is applause.

TEMPLE:	I'm going upstairs to see Bellamy – I shan't be long.
FORBES:	Yes, all right.

The dance orchestra starts again.

FADE the orchestra very slowly.

CUT TO: Upstairs at the Machicha Club. Outside Bellamy's Office.

TEMPLE knocks on the door.

BELLAMY: (*From inside: nervously*) Who is it?

TEMPLE opens the door.

TEMPLE: Can I come in?

BELLAMY: Who ... Oh, hello, Temple! Yeah, sure, sure ... come in.

TEMPLE closes the door behind him.

TEMPLE: (*Faintly amused*) What's the matter, Mr Bellamy? You sound nervous.

BELLAMY: Nervous? Are you kiddin'? I'm like a jelly in a high wind. Ever since you made that crack about Belasco being here at the Machicha.

TEMPLE: But he is here, I've seen him.

BELLAMY: Yeah, I know, I know, that's why I'm nervous!

TEMPLE: You know, Bellamy, I've got a feeling that you're not quite so tough as you're painted!

BELLAMY: Compared with guys like Belasco, I'm a violet, and I don't care who knows it! (*Temple laughs*) Can I get you a drink?

TEMPLE: Are you having one?

BELLAMY: What do you think?

BELLAMY mixes some drinks.

TEMPLE: (*Casually*) Do you mind if I have a look at that periscope gadget of yours?

BELLAMY: Go ahead.

TEMPLE turns the table over and moves it round.

TEMPLE: You know this is an awfully good idea of yours, Bellamy. You can see the whole of the restaurant.

BELLAMY: (*Joining TEMPLE at the periscope*) Yeah, and on a clear day you can see practically the whole of Scotland Yard! Here's your drink.

TEMPLE: Thanks.

BELLAMY: You see that man standing over there?

TEMPLE: Yes.

BELLAMY: Flatfoot. (*TEMPLE laughs*) You see that guy drinking ginger ale? Flatfoot. Turn it around.

TEMPLE turns the table round.

BELLAMY: D'you notice the big guy?

TEMPLE: The one in tails?

BELLAMY: Yeah, the one in tails, so help me!

TEMPLE: I take it you recognise Divisional-Inspector Ronson?

BELLAMY: Recognise him? Who wouldn't recognise him? He doesn't even deceive the cigarette girl. O.K., turn it around!

TEMPLE turns the table round again.

BELLAMY: Isn't that Sir Graham Forbes?

TEMPLE: Yes.

BELLAMY: Say, where's Perry? Oh, there he is! I thought he'd be somewhere around. (*He turns the table*) And there's your French friend, do you see him?

TEMPLE: Kaufman, yes, I see him.

BELLAMY: You know, if you ask me, I think that guy's a bit of a mystery. You know, I can hardly believe he's a detective. He doesn't talk like one, he doesn't act like one, he doesn't even dress like one!

TEMPLE: Perhaps he's a very good detective, Mr Bellamy.

BELLAMY: Yeah. (*Impressed*) Could be! Maybe you've got something there!

TEMPLE and BELLAMY laugh.

BELLAMY: Temple …

TEMPLE: Yes?

BELLAMY: (*Hesitantly*) … Where's Dr Belasco?

TEMPLE: Dr Belasco?

BELLAMY: Yes. Point him out to me on the periscope.

TEMPLE: Well, I'm afraid I can't very well do that.

BELLAMY: Why not?

TEMPLE: Well, you see, he just doesn't happen to be in the restaurant.

BELLAMY: Well, where is he? You said he was here! You said he was here at the Machicha.

TEMPLE: Oh, he's here all right. As a matter of fact, he's standing right beside me.

BELLAMY: Right beside … are you crazy? Why, I'm the only person that's standing right beside you … You don't think that I'm Dr Belasco?

TEMPLE: Aren't you, Mr Bellamy?

BELLAMY: Are you nuts, why – (*He stops*) What makes you think I'm Belasco?

TEMPLE: Two nights ago, I made a phone call from here to Sir Graham Forbes. I told him to follow a taxi that intended to take Steve and me to a shop owned by one of your men – a man by the name of Abel Dunne. You overheard that phone call, Bellamy, and shot the driver of the taxi so that he shouldn't lead Sir Graham to the address in Layman Street.

BELLAMY: Go on.

222

TEMPLE:	When David Nelson got ambitious and decided to leave the Belasco set-up, you fixed his car –
BELLAMY:	That's a lie!
TEMPLE:	– you fixed his car and then conveniently turned up at the scene of the accident in order to divert suspicion.
BELLAMY:	That's a dirty lie!
TEMPLE:	At the beginning you intended to throw suspicion on to Mrs Forester – that's why you told me that Joseph had asked you about Dr Belasco. You suggested to Mrs Forester that she should get in touch with Abel Dunne regarding the Hamish-Frinton papers. Later, however, you switched suspicion on to Worth and told Sir Graham Forbes a completely false story about Worth visiting the Machicha.
BELLAMY:	Worth did visit the Machicha! You know darn well he did! He told me to take £900 down to Reiford. What are you talking about? Didn't we go there? Didn't we find –
TEMPLE:	The dead body of Abel Dunne – and you know why, Bellamy? Because the poor devil had already served his purpose, because –
BELLAMY:	Are you suggesting that I shot Dunne?
TEMPLE:	Of course, you did! And shall I tell you how? You walked across to the cottage; when you were about twenty yards away you took a revolver from your pocket and fired a shot into the ground. That was the shot Sir Graham and I heard, that was

223

supposed to have killed Abel Dunne. You put the revolver back into your pocket, dashed up to the cottage, peered through the window, waved to Sir Graham and me, and then walked into the cottage, fitted a silencer to your revolver and shot the poor devil dead.

BELLAMY picks up a lamp and swings it at TEMPLE.

BELLAMY: Why, you cunning swine, I'll ...

TEMPLE: Put that lamp down, put that ... Oh!!!

BELLAMY catches Temple on the back of the head: there is a dull thud, and TEMPLE falls. BELLAMY rushes to the door, opens it, slams it behind him and turns a key in the lock. TEMPLE rises, groaning slightly. He moves to the door and tries it.

TEMPLE: What a fool, what a complete idiot! Oh, my head! (*He tries the door again*) What happened, what ...

TEMPLE pulls himself together and starts shouting and banging on the door.

TEMPLE: Open the door! Open the door! Sir Graham! Perry! For heaven's sake open the door!

TEMPLE commences to throw his weight against the door, breaking it down.

CUT TO: The Machicha Club Restaurant.

FADE UP of excited voices. The guests at the Machicha are under the impression that a police raid is in progress. Suddenly, the voice of INSPECTOR PERRY dominates the scene.

PERRY: Ladies and gentlemen – please! Please!

The voices die down.

PERRY:	There's no cause for alarm, the club is not being raided. Now kindly return to your tables! (*Aside*) Start the orchestra and keep playing!

The dance orchestra starts, as TEMPLE arrives, out of breath.

PERRY:	Have you seen Ronson, sir?
TEMPLE:	Yes, he's checked on the goods entrance but it's no use, I'm afraid.
PERRY:	It's beginning to look pretty black, sir.
TEMPLE:	Here's Sir Graham!
FORBES:	Carter's been on the Bruton Street entrance all the time – he's not seen him!
TEMPLE:	It's nearly fifteen minutes ago, Sir Graham! If he's not in the building, then by God he's miles away by now!
FORBES:	He must be in the building, Temple!
PERRY:	Unless there's a concealed entrance on to the roof, sir, and he's made a dash for it across –
TEMPLE:	(*Interrupting PERRY*) Here's Kaufman.
KAUFMAN:	You're wanted on the telephone, Temple – it's your wife.
TEMPLE:	Steve?
KAUFMAN:	She sounded most perturbed – she told me to tell you it was urgent.
TEMPLE:	But I don't understand how the devil she … Which box is it?
KAUFMAN:	The one in the hall – near the cloakroom.
TEMPLE:	(*Racing away*) Thanks.

CUT TO: The Machicha Club Phone Box.
TEMPLE lifts the telephone receiver. The conversation is swift, tense, and very urgent.

TEMPLE: (*On the phone*) Is that you, Steve?

STEVE: (*On the other end*) Paul, listen, this has got
               to be quick. I'm in a desperate hurry,
               darling! Now listen! I left the flat about
               half an hour after you and Sir Graham –

TEMPLE: But you couldn't have done. I gave you a
               sleeping draught.

STEVE: You don't think I fell for that corny old
               gag. I emptied it into the flower vase.

TEMPLE: Well, I'm –

STEVE: Paul, do listen. I took a taxi down to the
               Machicha Club. Just as I arrived, I saw
               Bellamy climbing down one of the fire-
               escapes. He had a car waiting for him.

TEMPLE: Did you follow him?

STEVE: That's what I'm trying to tell you, I –

TEMPLE: Steve, did you follow him?

STEVE: Yes, he's on the 10.15 to Benworth – it
               leaves Euston in exactly four minutes!

TEMPLE: The 10.15 to … oh, my lord that's – Steve,
               where are you? Where are you speaking
               from?

STEVE: I'm at Euston – I'm just getting on the
               train!

TEMPLE: For heaven's sake don't do that, he's
               extremely dangerous!

STEVE: Darling, listen! The train stops at
               Bletchdale, that's about thirty-five miles
               down the line, if you get in the car there's
               just a chance …

TEMPLE: O.K! O.K. Steve – I'll make it. Don't
               worry, darling, I'll make it!

Play Incidental Music.

MIX TO: TEMPLE's Car, travelling at very high speed.
MUSIC UP.

MIX TO: A Train Compartment.
The train is travelling at a moderate speed.
FADE MUSIC.
The sliding door of the compartment opens. TEMPLE enters.

STEVE: Paul! Paul, I've been so worried …
TEMPLE: Now just take it easy, Steve. Where is he?
STEVE: He's in the next compartment, darling.
TEMPLE: You're sure?
STEVE: Yes.
TEMPLE: Is he alone?
STEVE: Yes.
TEMPLE: He hasn't seen you?
STEVE: No, I was terribly careful.
TEMPLE: Good girl, Steve.
STEVE: What are you going to do?

TEMPLE passes a revolver to STEVE.

TEMPLE: Take this revolver – follow close behind
              me – and keep me covered.
STEVE: Yes, all right …

TEMPLE opens the compartment door. They move along to the next compartment. TEMPLE throws open the door, taking BELLAMY completely by surprise.

BELLAMY: Temple! What are you doing here!
TEMPLE: Don't move, Bellamy! Don't move!
STEVE: Paul, what's he doing?!
TEMPLE: Bellamy, I warn you, if you move, I'll
              shoot.

BELLAMY moves to the other door and starts to try to open it.

STEVE: Paul, he's trying to get out the other side!

227

TEMPLE: Bellamy, don't be a damn fool – stay where you are!

BELLAMY: O.K. – go ahead and shoot! Go on!

TEMPLE: I warn you – move away from that door!

BELLAMY throws open the carriage door. A rush of wind and the sound of the track is heard.

BELLAMY: O.K., shoot!

STEVE: Paul, he's going to jump!

TEMPLE: Bellamy, I'm warning you for the last time – move away from that door!

BELLAMY: You haven't got the nerve to shoot, Temple! You know darn well you haven't … argh!

BELLAMY suddenly slips, his body dangling out of the door, his hands barely hanging on.

STEVE: Paul, he's slipping!

TEMPLE: Bellamy!

STEVE: Paul, catch him! Get hold of his coat, darling!

BELLAMY gives another cry of alarm; he realises now that he is falling. TEMPLE tries to hold him. Then the sound of a train approaching on the other line is heard …

STEVE: Listen! There's another train coming! There's another train coming!

TEMPLE fails to hold BELLAMY, who falls, uttering a quick, terrifying shriek as the second train thunders by. Play Incidental Music.

CUT TO: The TEMPLES' Lounge.

TEMPLE, STEVE and SIR GRAHAM are having tea in front of the fire.

TEMPLE: (*Brightly; pleased with himself*) Have another cake, Sir Graham.

FORBES: (*Tempted*) No, thank you, Temple. I really ought to be making a move.

TEMPLE: Nonsense! Another cup of tea, darling!

STEVE: (*Eating*) You know, there's something I don't quite understand, Paul –

TEMPLE: Yes, there's something I don't understand either – why do you always have to eat with your mouth full!

STEVE: Well, you can't eat with your mouth empty!

TEMPLE: I mean talk with –

STEVE: (*Laughing at PAUL*) We know what you mean, darling!

They all laugh.

FORBES: We checked up on Lord Craymore, Temple. He apparently worked for Belasco and like Harry Marx suddenly decided to double-cross him. Oh, incidentally, the Greenchurch people have picked up a man called Allen – he's the fellow that Worth told us about. It looks as if he's the man that beat up Braddock and, acting on Belasco's instructions –

TEMPLE: Dumped him at Mrs Forester's?

FORBES: Yes.

STEVE: The thing I don't understand is why Bellamy went down to Reiford? Surely, if he wanted to get rid of Abel Dunne he –

TEMPLE: Don't overlook the fact that Belasco – or Bellamy if you like, Steve – was very sure of himself. He looked upon the trip to Reiford simply as a means of pulling the wool over our eyes.

FORBES: Exactly. Also, I think he felt that even if we did tend to suspect him, that trick outside the cottage would convince us that he couldn' possibly have shot Dunne and consequently … couldn't possibly be Belasco.

TEMPLE: Yes. You know, Sir Graham, Belasco was a pretty shrewd bird. When I arranged for Mrs Forester to disappear and pretend to be dead –

FORBES: (*Drily*) In order to convince me that she wasn't Dr Belasco!

TEMPLE: (*A little laugh*) Yes; I felt confident that he'd switch suspicion on to someone else – as a matter of fact, I rather favoured Kaufman. But you saw what happened! He saw through my little ruse and actually switched suspicion on to himself!

STEVE: You mean the silver pencil?

TEMPLE: Yes. Quite frankly, that rather shook me – I began to wonder if I was on the wrong track. As soon as I realised that Bellamy had provided himself with a first-class alibi – too good an alibi – I saw what he was getting at.

STEVE: He was in fact trying to convince you that Belasco had switched suspicion on to Bellamy! That's why one of his men planted the pencil at the warehouse.

TEMPLE: Exactly!

FORBES: Oh, he was a shrewd bird all right, make no mistake about that. (*Rising*) Well – I expect you're glad it's all over, Steve.

TEMPLE: I know I am!

FORBES: (*A little surprised*) You are?

TEMPLE: Rather! From now on, Sir Graham, I'm going to sit back with my feet on the mantelpiece and, as Sam Dodsworth would say, think of nothing more important than the temperature of the beer.

FORBES: But that's exactly what you said after the Gregory Affair!

STEVE: Word for word.

TEMPLE: Is it?

FORBES: Of course, it is!

TEMPLE: (*Genuinely surprised*) Well, I'm damned.

FORBES and STEVE are laughing at TEMPLE.

STEVE: Oh, darling!

TEMPLE: Yes, well you can laugh – you can laugh yourselves silly. But this time I'm serious – really serious! I'm absolutely, positively, definitely, once-and-for-all, finished with this sort of thing!

STEVE: Until the next time.

A pause.

TEMPLE: Until the next time.

They all start to laugh.

Closing Music.

THE END

Paul Temple and a Dr Belasco
by Francis Durbridge

One morning, about two or three weeks after I had started work on *Paul Temple and Steve,* I received a telephone call from Martyn C. Webster, who has been responsible for the production of all the Paul Temple plays and is of course producing the new serial.

I was actually having a bath when the telephone rang and I slipped a towel over my shoulders, slipped on my dressing-gown, slipped on my slippers – very nearly slipped on the soap – and dashed into my study.

Martyn's voice said: "I'm sorry to disturb you, old man, but it's rather urgent. Will you ring the Editor of Radio Times? He would like you to write an article on the new Paul Temple serial. He suggests that you write about nine hundred words describing exactly how you thought of the play."

I said: "I never tell people how I think of my plays!"

Martyn's voice said: "Well, this time you've got to make an exception! Think it over."

I thought it over. I thought it over for twenty-four hours. Then, quite suddenly, I made up my mind to spill the beans.

It all started on the afternoon of Wednesday January 15. I had an appointment during that afternoon: rather an important appointment. I kept the appointment and then, something around a quarter to four, I found myself sitting in a first-class railway carriage staring at a most bewitching L.M.S. photograph of Aberystwyth. I stared at the photograph for some considerable time and then suddenly, with a cry of alarm, I sprang to my feet.

It had dawned on me that I hadn't the slightest idea where I was going or what I was actually doing in the carriage.

I glanced at the rack above my head and there, to my astonishment, was a small leather suitcase bearing the initials 'P.T.'

The man sitting opposite me leant forward and said: "There's no need for alarm, my friend. Just sit down and relax." He was a rather pleasant-looking man and he spoke with a slight French accent.

I said: "I don't know whether I've lost my memory or not, sir, but quite frankly I don't know where I'm going."

The man made a little bow and said: "Permit me to introduce myself. My name is Philip Kaufman and I am attached to the Special Branch of the Criminal Investigation Department."

I raised my eyebrows, "Are we by any chance traveling together," I asked.

He nodded and flicked his cigarette lighter.

"We are going north," he said. "To interview a gentleman by the name of Mr David Nelson."

I said: "But this is silly. I've never even heard of a Mr David Nelson. Why should I want to interview a Mr David Nelson I've never even heard of?"

Kaufman said slowly: "Your joke has gone far enough, Mr Temple. You know as well as I do that in all probability David Nelson is none other than the notorious Dr Belasco."

"Dr Belasco!" I said. "Who on earth is Dr Belasco?"

Kaufman snapped: "Talk to the authorities in Copenhagen about Dr Belasco, Mr Temple! Talk to them in Oslo! In Stockholm! In Prague! Ask to see the Belasco dossier. There are precisely two hundred and seventy-nine closely typed pages dealing with the activities of Dr Belasco!"

"Yes, that's all very well," I said. "But – who – is – Dr Belasco?"

There was a moment's pause before Kaufman spoke.

"We don't know, Mr Temple," he said at length. "It might be David Nelson, it might be Henry Worth, it might be Mrs Forester, it might be Joseph, or it might even be Ed Bellamy." He looked extremely serious as he added, "Your wife of course suspects me!"

I began to feel hot under the collar and distinctly uncomfortable.

"Look here," I said, "there seems to be some sort of a mistake. In the first place my name is not Paul Temple. It's …"

Kaufman interrupted.

"You must understand, Mr Temple, that Belasco doesn't create crime. He organises crime: organises the existing crime, as it were. There is of course a subtle difference."

Suddenly I remembered my wallet and pulled it from my inside pocket. "This ought to convince you that I'm not your precious Mr Temple!" I said desperately. I opened the wallet and extracted a visiting card. Kaufman took it and smiled. "You appear to have quite a nice line in visiting cards, my friend," he said slowly.

He held the card towards me so that I could read it.

The card said: "Who is the notorious Dr Belasco?"

I dropped the wallet and closed my eyes. I suddenly felt rather sick. I could feel Kaufman pressing down on me. I had the strange feeling that he was trying to open my eyes.

Eventually I did open my eyes and the Dentist said: "Well, that won't trouble you again, old boy!"

He showed me the tooth.

I asked: "How long was I under the anaesthetic?"

The Dentist said: "Oh, not long. Why?"

"Did I behave all right?"

"Perfectly."

I said: "Well, I certainly know what my next play is going to be all about. I hope you'll listen to it."

"I'll make a point of it," said the Dentist and ushered me into the waiting room.

The rather pretty looking nurse said: "I'm afraid Dr Belasco has cancelled his appointment for Tuesday and Mrs Forester has postponed her extraction until Thursday."

The Dentist said: "What about Mr Worth?"

"He's coming at 5.15," said the nurse.

I gasped.

"Look here," I said. "You don't happen to have a patient called Kaufman by any chance?"

The Dentist nodded towards the nurse. "No," he said, "but this is Miss Kaufman."

And that is how I thought of the story of *Paul Temple and Steve*. At least, I *think* that's how I thought of the story. At any rate, so far as the Editor of the Radio Times is concerned, THAT'S MY STORY!

Printed in Great Britain
by Amazon

78766707R00146